THE DISPUTE AT THE FAIR

A RAZZY CAT COZY MYSTERY BOOK #16

COURTNEY MCFARLIN

D1713761

1

*T*here's something special about waking up on a lazy Saturday morning, when you know you don't need to be anywhere, and the entire day is stretching ahead of you. Add in bonus points when you know the weather is going to be great, and you've got the makings of a wonderful weekend.

I snuggled under the comforter and wished today was one of those days. It was a Saturday, but it would not be a lazy day. In fact, I was the only one still in bed, and the delectable smell of coffee coming from the kitchen did nothing to tempt me out from underneath the covers.

I'd worked late the night before, staying up to file a story for The Post, the newspaper where I covered the crime beat. A string of recent bank robberies had ended spectacularly, and I'd rushed to be one of the first members of the press to file my story. I'd only been asleep for a few hours, and was desperate for just a little more shut eye.

"Mama, come on, it's time to get up."

I huddled further into the bed as Razzy, my Ragdoll cat, stomped her way across the bed, making a beeline for me. There was no way I was going to fool her.

"Just five more minutes?"

The bed sank even further, as our other Ragdoll, Rudy, joined us. As always, he was chock full of energy, raring to go. A paw snaked down in front of my face and gently pulled the covers down, revealing a set of beautiful blue eyes in his smoky brown face.

"Ben's making breakfast and it smells amazing," the young cat said before bouncing around on the bed and careening into the hall, skittering as he went.

Oh, to be a cat, full of energy. Razzy snuggled into my side, purring.

"He's making your favorite breakfast."

I cracked an eye and propped myself up on my elbow.

"French toast and bacon?"

"Yep. He's even making a special fruit thing to go on the top."

The thought of Ben's French toast with homemade strawberry glaze made my mouth water and convinced me to face the day. I sat up and stroked Razzy's sleek brown and cream fur, marveling at how her coat shone in the sunshine streaming in through the bedroom window.

"You're a gorgeous cat, you know that?"

"Of course. That's a given."

"And humble, too," I said with a snort. "Okay, I'm up. Let's go see what Ben's up to in the kitchen. Maybe I can help."

The look on her face spoke volumes about what she thought about that idea. Razzy jumped off the bed, leaving me to follow her at a much more sedate pace. Gus, Ben's Maine Coon cat, met me in the hall, his tufted ears perked.

"Hey, lady. There you are. Come on, breakfast is ready."

I was escorted to the kitchen by my feline honor guard, where I found Ben drizzling strawberry glaze over a pile of French toast. Be still my beating heart.

His gorgeous green eyes crinkled into a smile as he heard me approach and he turned, grabbed a cup of coffee, and pressed it into my hand before leaning forward to kiss my cheek. Yep, this man was a keeper.

"Good morning, sunshine. What time did you make it to bed last night? I didn't even hear you come in."

I yawned widely before taking my first sip of coffee.

"Three-ish. Mmm, this is good. Is that the new brand we just bought?"

"It is. I liked it, too. Breakfast is almost ready. So, tell me about the robbers. How did they catch them?"

Ben used to be a homicide detective on the Golden Hills police force and recently started his own detective agency. While it had started slowly, after he'd solved a big case with cartel connections, his phone had been ringing off the hook.

"It was just like you thought. A teller at the latest bank that was hit came forward and admitted it was her boyfriend and his friends. Apparently, she didn't know they were going to target her bank. I'm not sure I'm buying it, though. It sounds like she's trying to save her own skin."

"Hmm. Most likely. All right, everyone, breakfast is served."

The cats scrambled towards the dining table, taking their places on their seats. Most cats ate in bowls on the floor, but not our brood. Razzy, in particular, insisted on being civilized and eating at the table. The two boys followed her lead.

Ben handed me a heaping plate, and I shuffled after him, breathing in the strawberry vanilla goodness as the steam rose from my plate. This was just what I needed.

Fortified with sugar and caffeine, my outlook immediately brightened. By the time I was done scarfing down breakfast, I was more than ready to take on the day.

"Oh, I talked to Eden. She's having a rough time up there. If I have some time later, I'll need to run some background searches for her. We need to get up there and see her. It's been too long."

Ben smiled as he finished his cup of coffee and passed out the little pieces of bacon he'd saved for the cats.

"You were all very patient. Well done. I wouldn't mind taking a brief vacation soon," Ben said. "We should go up and see her. We could stay in a cabin again, just like last time."

Gus puffed out his furry chest proudly, always tickled when he made Ben happy. Rudy stared longingly at my plate, where some of the strawberry glaze remained.

"Can I try that? It looks so good."

His eyes were enormous in his little face and my heart melted, like it always did. I dipped my finger in the glaze and held it out for him.

"Only a little. Each of you can try it, if you'd like."

Razzy and Gus watched in fascination as Rudy sniffed my finger before delicately licking up the glaze. Apparently, he was the guinea pig today. It didn't take long for the two of them to crowd around as soon as they saw how much he enjoyed it.

"Delicious," Razzy said before washing her face with a snowy white paw. "What's on the schedule today?"

That was my little girl. Ever the task master. Ben smiled and leaned back in his chair.

"I've got to meet my new client. He's a vendor at the fair down in Canyon Falls. Hannah, do you want to come?"

I longingly thought of our plush bed, but I nodded, anyway. This case of Ben's was intriguing, and I was more than happy to tag along.

"I'm up for it. What's the case about again?"

"Burt Younkin is his name. He runs the Green Chile Experience stand at all the local fairs. He's convinced one of his competitors is sabotaging him and he's paying me to get the evidence to prove himself right."

"Huh. I can't imagine it being that big of a deal, but if he's willing to pay someone to help him, I won't knock it."

"He even offered extra pay since I'll need to work weekends until it's solved. Plus, we can eat for free at his stand."

I perked up, even though I'd just demolished my sizable breakfast.

"Really? What's he sell?"

"Burgers, burritos, you name it. If you can put green chiles on it, I guess he sells it. Knowing the locals around here, probably a few things that shouldn't have green chiles on them are on the menu, too."

He wasn't wrong. This part of Colorado was green chile crazy. I was a transplant from South Dakota, but I'd quickly become a fan of the savory treat soon after I'd moved here for college.

"Cool. Maybe I can find some stuff for the apartment while you're looking around. There's usually a bunch of different vendors at events like this. What's the theme for this year's fair?"

"It's the Spring Fling. I looked into a little last night while I was waiting for you to come to bed. It looks like fun."

"I wish we could go," Razzy said, looking down at the table. "We could help you sniff out some clues and solve the case faster."

My heart sank as I looked at her sad expression. Our cats loved nothing more than solving mysteries, and they hated being kept away from the action. Razzy was used to going to work with me nearly every day, and the boys typically went with Ben when they could.

"I know, sweetheart. There's going to be too many people around, though, and it's not safe. And the temps are supposed to be pretty warm today. You guys would roast in the car, and that's not safe either. I'm sorry."

She heaved a sigh and hopped down from her chair, trudging into the living room with heavy paws. Gus and Rudy looked at each other before following. I glanced at Ben, but he shook his head slightly. I nodded, agreeing that we just couldn't risk it, even though I know it made our cats miserable. Their safety was way more important. An idea popped into my head and I smiled as I looked over at Razzy.

"Tell you what, guys. We'll find some cool stuff to bring home, and I'll record everything on my phone, so it will be like you're really there with us. We can watch it as soon as we get home."

"Can we have fried chicken and all the fixings for supper?"

She drove a hard bargain, but there was no way Ben or I could resist her. I smothered a smile and nodded.

"Of course."

"Hooray," Rudy said, launching himself off the couch to run around the living room. "Mashed taters and corn!"

COURTNEY MCFARLIN

It took very little to make them happy. I grabbed Ben's plate and loaded the dishwasher while he cleaned up the mess from breakfast. Once he was done, he planted a kiss on the top of my head before going back to get ready for the day. While I waited for my turn to shower, I grabbed my phone and joined the cats on the couch.

My boss, Tom Anderson, had emailed me at the crack of dawn, praising my latest piece on the bank robbers, but that was the only email that wasn't spam. I pulled up the website for the Spring Fling fair and read a little about the scheduled events.

"Look at this, guys, there's a cooking competition for the food vendors. The Green Chile Experience is listed, and about five other vendors. I wonder which one is the one they suspect of sabotage?"

Razzy peered over my elbow to look at my phone before giving a kitty shrug.

"Hard to tell. Ooh, that barbecue vendor looks interesting. Maybe I should rethink that whole fried chicken thing."

I stroked her little head while she joined me in reading about the fair. By the time Ben was out of the shower, she was back in good spirits, giving me orders about the things she wanted to see in my video.

"Oh, and make sure you get good shots of the goats, if there are any. Especially the baby goats. They're hilarious."

"Yes, my queen," I said, smiling over at Ben as he joined us.

His close-cropped hair was still a little wet on top, and he looked better than any man had a right to, considering he was wearing just a regular t-shirt and jeans. Yep, I was a lucky woman. I put down my phone and got ready to shower, humming as I turned on the water.

It might not be the lazy Saturday I wanted, but it was sure looking like it was going to be an interesting day. I hadn't been to a fair since I was a little girl, and my parents took me to the county fair in our little community. As I remembered it, I'd had a lot of fun, and I couldn't wait to experience this one with Ben.

With any luck, this case would be an open and shut one, and we'd have the rest of the weekend free to spoil our cats and enjoy the beautiful weather.

2

Once we'd parked in the fairgrounds, and began our dusty trek to where all the action was centered, the smells of the multitude of fried delicacies were tickling my nose.

"Ooh, do you think they have funnel cakes?" I said, bouncing a little. "I haven't had a good funnel cake in years."

Ben smiled and shrugged.

"Maybe? What's a funnel cake? And we just had breakfast."

"You're kidding, right? Breakfast is irrelevant when you're going to the fair. It's like a law or something that you have to get a bunch of junk food. I've even heard of some fairs where they have deep fried candy bars."

"That does not sound appetizing. I can't say I've ever had anything called a funnel cake, though."

"You're right, but funnel cakes are amazing. They're like deep fat fried pockets of angel kissed air, dusted lightly with powdered sugar."

Ben chuckled and leaned close to kiss the top of my head.

"I'll make sure you get one and maybe we can share."

I narrowed my eyes and shook my finger at him.

"I don't care how sweet you are. You can get your own. Where's your client going to be?"

Ben searched the row of vendors and pointed towards the end.

"It looks like the food stands are all back there. Let's go meet this Mr. Younkin and see what he has to say."

I trotted along happily, recognizing many of the same styles of vendors from the fairs of my youth. A saddle maker was working behind his booth, while at another, someone was giving a demonstration on calf roping. The smells wafting from the other end of the midway reminded me that there were some animals here as well. Hopefully, I'd be able to get a good video of the goats for the cats.

Ben came to a stop outside a colorful food truck, painted in varying shades of green, yellow, and red. I sniffed and nearly swooned as the smell of roasted green chiles filled the air.

"Howdy, welcome to the Green Chile Experience. How hot do you like it?"

Ben blinked at the older man standing in the food truck's window.

"I'm here to see Burt Younkin. My name's Ben Walsh."

"Oh, howdy Walsh. One second, lemme get my grandson to watch the truck. Gerald! Gerald! Get your skinny butt out here and watch the front. I've got business I need to do."

A rail-thin teenager with pale reddish hair poked his head around the side of the truck. His skin was mottled with freckles and pimples, and flushed red as soon as he saw us.

"Sorry, grandpa. I'm here. I was just..."

"You were looking at that pretty little girl who's helping Freya. Don't even try to deny it. Now, get behind here and get to work. Kids these days," Burt said, as he lumbered down the stairs to the outside.

I got my first good look at Burt Younkin as he stood in front of us. He was much shorter than Ben and much wider. His graying hair was fighting a losing battle with his scalp under his hair net. His bulging eyes were a startling blue.

"Nice to meet you, Mr. Walsh. I'm sure glad you came out today. I found that evidence I was telling you about."

Ben looked around the midway that was slowly filling up with people and shifted his feet.

"Is there somewhere we can talk about this privately?"

Burt shot a look across the way, and his eyes filled with malice.

"Not a bad idea. Come on back here, I've got some chairs set up in a break-area for when the truck gets too hot."

I paused and looked over to where Burt had glared. Right across the way was a barbecue stand, but it was strangely empty. Most of the booths had employees and owners scrambling around, getting ready for the day, but the Pit Stop BBQ stand was quiet. I shook my head and hurried after Ben.

"Take a seat, miss," Burt said, pointing towards a rickety lawn chair. "I was just telling your man here all about Tex Randolph and his sneaky ways."

I sank into the chair with a wince as it gave an alarming creak. Ben, who was well over six feet and solidly built, looked incredibly uncomfortable in his chair.

"You've known Tex for how long?"

"Oh, heck, over twenty years now. Do you know how the fair circuits work?"

"I don't."

"Well, every spring and summer, all of us vendors go from place to place, selling our wares, just like they used to do in the wild west. We hit up major festivals, too. Anywhere where we can make a buck, you'll find us. It's competitive and hard work, but once you start, you can't stop. I swore I was only gonna do it for a summer, and that was back when I was young Gerald's age. Look at me now."

Burt folded his hands over his substantial middle and beamed proudly at us.

"That's quite an accomplishment," I said. "Have you always been a food vendor?"

"Yes, ma'am. My special Green Chile recipe was handed down to me by my grandmother. It's an old family secret. That's what makes what Tex is doing all the worse. He knows better, but I suppose the lure of the prize has finally gotten to his judgment."

"Prize?" Ben asked, shifting his weight forward on the chair.

"Yessir. The Spring Fling's annual cook-off is tonight. Every year, all of us face off against each other to compete for different categories. It includes everything from sides to the main course. Now, at the other festivals, Tex and I split up the winnings, but this one? I've always won the Spring Fling. Twenty years in a row."

"And you believe Tex is trying to sabotage you?"

"Yessir. And that's not all," Burt said, leaning forward as well and lowering his voice. "He's stooped so low that he's stealing my ingredients to make sure I can't win. Not only that, he's even taken my prize set of grill tools. My daddy hand carved those handles for me when I was just a pup."

"Why would he take something so distinctive? Wouldn't that be a clear giveaway of his guilt?" I asked.

"Oh, I don't think he's going to use them. If you ask me, he's taken them and hidden them away to get me off my game. It won't work, but I know how old Tex thinks. He'll stash them somewhere and say I'm getting old and forgot where I put them. It's gone too far, though. I know he's guilty, but I need you to prove it."

"How much is the prize?" Ben asked.

"This year it's gone up quite a bit. Ten grand to the winner of the main dish category. I'm certain I'm a shoo-in, but you never know."

"What ingredients have been stolen?"

"You name it," Burt said, spreading his hands wide. "My signature chile sauce, my spices, and I think he even tried to get his hands on the recipe. Gerald said he was snooping around, but I wasn't born yesterday. I keep nothing written. It's all up here."

He tapped the side of his head and nodded. I didn't know the lives of fair vendors were so exciting. It sounded like quite a lot went on behind the cheerful facades of the food trucks.

"I emailed over the contract, but I have a printed copy in my car for you to sign," Ben said. "If you want to go ahead, that is. I'll need a retainer, but I can do a payment plan if that fits your budget better."

"Nah, I'll pay cash on the nose," Burt said, heaving himself upward with a grunt. "I prefer it that way. Go get your paper and then once it's all signed, you can try one of my chile burgers. On the house, of course. I want to make sure you're fueled up. I need you to find that evidence before tonight."

Ben stood and shook hands with Burt before turning to me.

"Do you want to come with me back to the car?"

"No, I think I'll hang around here and do a little preliminary snooping, if that's okay?"

"Sure, I'll just be a few minutes."

Ben nodded at Burt before jogging off, his long strides quickly taking him from sight. I turned back to Burt.

"Do you have a picture of your tools?"

"Of course. Come on into the kitchen. I'll have you put one of these on first, though. No offense, but I can't risk my clean kitchen."

He handed me a crumpled hair net that felt sticky over to me and I grimaced as I eased it over my hair. He led the way into the tight quarters of the food truck, where Gerald was sweating over a vat of green chile sauce.

"Here you go," Burt said, gesturing to the back side of the narrow kitchen.

Up on the wall, behind the fryer, liberally speckled with grease, were a row of photographs, all featuring Burt Younkin, wearing his signature hairnet and a huge smile. He pulled one off the wall and handed it to me.

"This was last year's Spring Fling. If you'll look, right there on the side is my stand with all my tools. It's not the best picture, but you'll be able to see the carving."

I peered closely at the picture and caught myself making a pinching movement on the glass to enlarge it. Burt guffawed next to me, slapping me across the back heartily.

"I've seen Gerald do the same thing. Dang devices these days. Can you see them, though?"

I squinted and made out the shape of what looked like a pig's head on one tool.

"They're all carved into animal heads?"

"Yes, ma'am. A pig, a cow, and a sheep. Now, I use little mutton, but I make some mean smoked pork, marinated with green chile sauce, and then doused in it when it goes onto the bun. It's my second best seller, next to the burgers."

I handed the photo back and sniffed appreciatively.

"Well, whatever your recipe is, this all smells delicious."

"You can have your pick. There's your man, now. You gotta pen for me, son? I don't have one handy."

Ben nodded, and we headed out of the narrow kitchen to the obvious relief of the sweating Gerald. I squinted in the bright sun and looked across. The Pit Stop was still empty. I tilted my head to the side and looked at all the other vendors. Sure enough, they were bustling around, just like Burt and Gerald. I glanced over my shoulder at Ben.

"I'll be right back. I just want to check on something."

Ben gave me an absentminded wave, and I headed across the midway. The truck next to the Pit Stop was selling stuffed baked potatoes, and the owner gave me a friendly smile as I approached.

"Wanna try one of our taters? I saw you over there with Burt. We use his special sauce on our Colorado Chile Tater."

"Maybe later," I said, smiling at the freckled woman behind the counter. "I was curious about the shop next door. Is it always that quiet before the lunch rush?"

"Tex? Now that you say something, that is odd. He's always around, from sunup to sundown. In fact, we have a little friendly competition most days about who can get set up first. Tex usually wins."

"It's been empty since we got here, about a half an hour ago," I said. "Do you think he's okay?"

"I sure hope so. Tex or his partner Pete's usually here. Let's go around back and see if they're out there. I'm Sheila, by the way."

"Hannah. Nice to meet you."

She came down the steps and led the way between the two food trucks. She turned the corner and shouted.

"Tex? You around?"

Silence greeted us. She scowled and waved at me to follow.

"Tex? You've got someone who wants to see you. Tex?"

She stopped dead in her tracks and gasped, her skin going so pale her freckles looked like they'd been drawn on with a sharpie.

"Oh my gosh. Tex!"

She moved forward, and I finally saw what she was looking at. A big man was lying face down on the ground, right behind the food truck. Sticking out of his back was a long metal rod, topped with a carved grinning pig's head. My breath whooshed out as Sheila turned her tear-streaked face towards me.

"He's dead. Someone murdered Tex."

I took a step back and held up a hand.

"Wait right there. My boyfriend used to be a cop. Touch nothing. You're sure he's dead? I'll go get Ben."

"No pulse. There's blood all around him," Sheila said, backhanding tears from her face as she looked closely at the weapon skewering Tex. "This belongs to..."

Our eyes met, and I realized that my hopes of a quick, open and shut case were completely dashed. I nearly fell over my feet as I moved to call for Ben. This did not look good for Burt Younkin.

3

$\mathcal{M}$y voice sounded strangled as I stood in the alleyway between the booths and called for Ben. He was just a few yards away, but his head was bent in conversation with Burt, and he obviously couldn't hear me. I glanced back at Sheila before hurrying across the midway.

"Ben!"

Ben's green eyes flared open as he spotted me and he raised an eyebrow before patting Burt's arm and heading towards me.

"Hannah, what's wrong?"

"You won't believe this. Come with me."

I took his arm and walked as quickly as I could without making a scene.

"Did you find a vendor with funnel cakes?"

"Not exactly. We need to call the police."

Ben's smile slid off his face as I hauled him around to the back of Tex's food truck and he spotted Sheila crouched next to Tex's massive frame.

"Oh, no."

I grimaced before pointing at Tex's back.

"It gets worse. He definitely didn't trip on that."

Ben approached Sheila and gently took her by the arm, helping her stand. She blinked several times as she looked at him.

"Who are you?"

"I'm Ben Walsh. I'm with Hannah. I need you to step away from the body and come over here while I call the police."

He led her away a few steps, and she stood there, arms wrapped around her middle, a dazed look on her face.

"Tex was always bigger than life. I can't believe it."

I came closer and put an arm around her shoulders, recognizing she was in shock as Ben called the police. I still wasn't completely used to the fact that he wasn't the police anymore.

"I'm so sorry, Sheila. The police will be here soon. Do you remember anyone coming past your stall in the past hour?"

Tears ran down her cheeks as she shook her head.

"I was so busy getting set up. I didn't really see anything that stood out, I guess. But you see the way we're parked. Anyone could come up from behind the trucks and we'd never see them."

She turned to point towards the open field behind us, and I grimaced. She was absolutely right. The bulk of the fairgrounds faced the other way. It would be all too easy to skirt the bustling grounds and approach from the back.

"When did you last see Tex?"

Sheila backhanded the tears from her cheeks and closed her eyes.

"It would have been when I first got here. Tex was playing his radio loud, like he always did. He loves... I mean... He loved old-style country music. You know, Waylon and Willy. I gained a whole new appreciation for them, thanks to Tex. I can't believe..."

She burst into tears again as I pulled her in for a hug and looked around the back of the truck. Everything was neatly stowed away, but there was no music playing. Hmm. Had Tex turned it off to speak to someone, or had the killer done that? Ben's face was grim as he came closer.

"They're on their way. Ray Weston is coming too. Do you remember him?"

I nodded as memories of the older police chief came back. He'd helped to save Ben's life when a murderous detective with ties to Blanco Ridge had tried to kill him to cover up his drug operation.

"I do. I didn't realize we were in his jurisdiction."

"There's been an upheaval with the sheriff's office, so Blanco Ridge has added this area to their beat."

"Wow, that can't be easy to cover. Oh, this is Sheila. She runs the potato food truck next door. She took me back here to meet Tex, and that's when we found him."

Sheila stepped back and nodded at Ben, carefully avoiding looking at Tex's body. She sniffed, and I dug in my bag, rooting around for some tissues. I handed one over and she smiled briefly, her freckles still stark in her pale face.

"Thank you. I just can't get over it. You don't think Burt did this, do you? I always thought their rivalry was friendly, but lately, it's taken a turn."

I flashed a look at Ben before darting my eyes towards the body.

"That's one of Burt's missing tools. He showed me a picture of the set a few minutes ago."

"This isn't good," he said, putting his hands on his hips. "Sheila, did you see anyone...?"

She blew her nose loudly and shook her head.

"I was just telling Hannah that I was busy getting set up. You two seem to know all the right questions to ask while I'm falling apart. She said you used to be a cop?"

"That's right. I'm a private detective now, and Hannah works for the Golden Hills Post as a reporter."

She wadded the tissue up and nodded.

"Makes sense I guess. I'm not used to this kind of violence."

I could hear sirens in the distance and took advantage of the time we had alone with her before the police arrived. Ray was a good cop, but I wasn't sure he'd appreciate us stomping all over his toes.

"You said the rivalry between Tex had gotten worse lately?"

She nodded and sent a mournful look in Tex's direction.

"I thought it was harmless. I guess not. They kept it mostly friendly, but over the past few months, Burt's been acting differently. He kept swearing things were going missing, only to find them later. I don't know if he's slipping, but it's been strange. Tex was always such a cheerful guy. He's been acting different, too. He'd always have time to chat, but lately, he's been closed off."

Ben's eyes met mine, and I saw the suspicion I was feeling about Burt Younkin mirrored in their green depths. Had Burt hired Ben to deflect suspicion, knowing all along he was going to kill his competitor? Somehow, that didn't add up. Burt hadn't struck as a man with anything to hide, but I'd only known him for half an hour. A man's voice called out from behind us.

"What's going on? Why is everyone back here?"

Ben stepped to the side, unblocking the view of Tex's body, and the man's face went the color of chalky clay. His hand shook as he held it to his chest. He was a tall, powerful looking man.

"Why are you just standing here? You've got to help him! Tex!"

"I'm sorry, but this is a crime scene," Ben said, grabbing the man by the shoulder to keep him from approaching the body. "We can't disturb any evidence. There's nothing we can do for him now."

He let out an anguished cry as Ben restrained him.

"No. No, it can't be. How? Why?"

"What's going on here?"

I turned and spotted a familiar man standing next to Chief Weston. I'd recognize Sam Trotter's bulky form anywhere. He looked more like a bodybuilder than a cop. The last time we'd met, he'd been a school resource officer, but here he was in plain clothes. Obviously, things had changed in Blanco Ridge from the last time we were there.

Ben nodded in Sam's direction.

"Trotter! I wasn't expecting you. How've you been?"

Sam's smile softened the harsh lines of his face and he ducked his head a little.

"Got promoted after the Samuels fiasco," he said, nodding towards the Chief. "I'm grateful, but I miss being at the school. How about you two, any wedding bells yet? Coleen was asking about you two a few weeks ago."

Ben flushed and looked away, not meeting my eyes.

"Not yet," he said, clearing his throat.

"So, what do we have here? I heard you left the force up there. What are you two doing down in our neck of the woods?" Chief Weston asked, giving me a gentle smile. "Hiya, Hannah."

"Hi Ray. It's good to see you, but I wish it was under different circumstances."

Sheila looked between us, her face crinkled in confusion.

"You all know each other?"

"It's a long story. Ben, why don't you tell them about Burt, and I'll take Sheila back to her food truck? I'm sure everyone's wondering where she is."

I led Sheila away and gave her the highlights of how we'd become friends with the officers at Blanco Ridge. She seemed to relax as I talked, and by the time she was behind her counter, a little color had come back to her face.

She looked around at all the toppings before casting a look across the midway. I followed her gaze and saw Burt Younkin, standing in front of his food truck, staring across towards Tex's truck. Sheila looked at me, eyes wide.

"Do you think he did it? You saw that skewer. It was his. I know it."

"He hired Ben to help with what he thought was sabotage, and he mentioned those tools went missing. I don't know when Tex was killed, but we were with him for at least half an hour. I don't think he did it, but it's possible. You know him better than I do. What do you think?"

I waited for her to respond while she kept looking over at Burt, wringing a towel between her hands.

"I don't know. I wouldn't think so. Burt's always seemed like a nice old granddad type, you know? Blustery, but good-hearted. I don't know if I'll ever get the image of poor Tex out of my head. If Burt didn't do it, who would?"

"Chief Weston and Detective Trotter are good cops. They'll figure it out. Do you have anyone helping you today?"

She dropped the towel and looked around the cramped interior of the food truck.

"No, it's just me. There's barely enough room for me, let alone anyone else. I don't know if I can do this today. Just act like everything is fine and serve people's food when one of my friends was murdered. But I need the money. Today's the opening day and will be the busiest. What do I do, Hannah?"

She covered her mouth, and her shoulders shook with quiet sobs. I stroked her back as I racked my brain to come up with a solution.

"Is there another vendor who could help?"

"Pete's helped me out before, when the heat got too much for me last summer. That's who showed up just now. He's Tex's partner. They're usually so busy they need one person manning the smoker and the other working up front. You know that's weird..."

I waited for a moment before prompting her.

"What's weird?"

"Where was Pete this morning? He always shows up at the same time as Tex. They're practically inseparable. Where was he? If he'd been around, I'm certain Tex would still be alive. Unless... No, I don't think he'd do it. But, Burt? I don't know..."

My wheels began turning as I watched Burt still staring at the barbecue truck. Had it all been an elaborate scene, staged to provide him with an alibi? By hiring Ben to find the missing tools, was he trying to cover up a crime he planned to commit?

Even though the interior of the potato truck was hot, an icy chill ran down my spine as I looked at Burt with fresh eyes. Was he capable of something so premeditated?

"Tell you what, Sheila. I need to go talk to Ben and the Chief. Then, I'll see if I can find someone to cover for you. I'm sure you'll need to give your statement, so stay put, okay? I'll be back in a few minutes."

I quickly hopped down the metal stairs that led out of the food truck, so focused on finding help for Sheila, I missed Burt approaching quickly. I nearly jumped out of my skin when he grabbed my arm.

"What's going on? Ben said he'd be right back. Is everything okay with Tex?"

I stammered for a moment as I searched his face. He didn't look like a murderer, but I'd been fooled before.

4

*B*urt shook my shoulder when I didn't respond. I snapped out of it and looked back over my shoulder. I would not be the one to tell him. If Burt had killed Tex, the way he reacted could be vital information to the police.

"You'd better come with me."

He gave me a strange look, but dropped his hand and waved me forward. I took a few steps towards the back of Tex's food truck and pulled up short. Pete was still standing there, talking to Ben and the Blanco Ridge police. His face was mottled red, and he was obviously furious. I forged ahead, hoping to catch some of what he was saying.

"What police force do we have when innocent people can be murdered, right at their place of business, and no one saw a thing?"

Spittle flew out of Pete's mouth, but Ray and Sam didn't back down. Ben spotted me and glanced over at Burt. I didn't miss the way his green eyes narrowed. Burt stepped forward.

"Pete, what the heck is going on? Did you say someone was murdered?"

The big man's face flushed even darker, and he stabbed his finger towards Burt before pushing past Ray.

"There he is! There's your murderer! Arrest this man immediately. There's only one person on this earth who wanted Tex dead, and he's right there."

Burt paled and lifted a shaky hand towards his heart.

"What? Tex is dead?"

"Oh, don't even play that game with me! I know you hated him and I know you're the one who stabbed him in the back. You've been doing it for years with your words, and now you've finally done it for real. For crying out loud, everyone knows who owns that stupid pig's head skewer!"

Pete moved towards Burt, his hands outstretched, while Burt stepped behind me. Ben hustled over, blocking me from the charging Pete. I snorted as Ray shouldered his way between the men and held up his hands. If Burt wanted to hide safely, he'd picked the wrong person to act as a human shield. The only way I cleared five feet was if my hair was up in a high ponytail. The absurdity didn't stop me from letting Ben pull me away.

"All right gentlemen, this is getting out of hand. Tensions are high and obviously everyone's upset. The coroner is almost here and until then, I can't have this scene any more contaminated than it is. Everyone needs to calm down."

Sam joined Ray, his bulky form acting as a wall between the two men. Ben stood, hands on hips, and watched Burt's face carefully. I edged closer to him.

"Tex is really dead? I don't... I can't..."

Ray grabbed Burt's arm as the man sagged on his feet.

"Is there a chair anywhere?" he barked, trying to keep Burt on his feet. "This man needs medical attention."

"The only medical attention he needs is the electric chair," Pete said with a snarl. "I won't rest until I prove you guilty, old man. You can count on it."

"I said that's enough!"

Ray's tone held enough steel to build a skyscraper, and Pete finally backed down. Sam grabbed a folding chair from behind the food truck and positioned it behind Burt, just in time to catch the older man as he sagged into it, face white as a sheet.

"He can't be dead. We're supposed to compete this afternoon. That's what we always do."

I pulled Ben away so we couldn't be overheard. Burt's actions had settled my creeping doubts.

"I know it looks bad, but I don't think he did it. If he's acting, he deserves an Oscar, an Emmy, and a Golden Globe."

"I agree. But unless they find evidence to back that up, it doesn't look good for him. You're sure it's his skewer?"

"Well, as positive as I can be. He showed me a picture of it right before I came back here. He said it was custom made. But if it was stolen, like he claimed, anyone could've done it."

Ben shook his head and glanced over to where Sam and Ray were interrogating Burt.

"He never filed a police report. I was going to suggest he do that. In fact, that's what we were talking about when you grabbed me. It's easy enough to say he only claimed they were stolen to throw suspicion away from him. I don't know, Hannah. It doesn't look good."

The coroner's white van slowly pulled into the small alley between the food trucks and I remembered my original errand.

"Sheila needs help running her food truck. I think she's in shock over finding Tex like that. She said Pete has helped her out before, but I don't think I want to ask him for anything. Not right now."

"Yeah, not a good idea. I have a feeling the festival might be shut down, but it's going to depend on what the owners say. Ray was on the phone with them before Burt showed up. I guess they're offsite, but they're on their way, too. This whole site is a murder scene, and we can't have people tromping through it."

The way he spoke reminded me of when he was running the homicide division in Golden Hills. Confident and in control. But this wasn't his crime scene. We'd lucked out that Ray and Sam were friendly to us, but would they appreciate us horning in on their investigation?

"Alright, Mr. Younkin. I've confirmed that the murder weapon belongs to you. I'm going to need you to come to the station," Sam said, helping Burt stand. "I'll escort you over to the patrol car."

"That's more like it. Why isn't he in cuffs?"

Pete's eyes held a malicious gleam as Burt struggled to his feet. I glanced at Ben, but he shook his head slightly, signaling he would not interfere. Burt looked around wildly, finally spotting us.

"I didn't do it. I'm an innocent man. I know what I said earlier, but I didn't do it! You've gotta help me clear my name, Walsh. I'm begging you."

Sam looked distinctly uncomfortable as he led Burt away. I wasn't sure how many murder cases he'd worked, but it probably never got easier. It wasn't easy for me seeing the look of anguish on Burt's face. We had to help him. Didn't we?

"Yeah, take him where he belongs. I can't wait to watch him burn."

Ray held up his hand and looked at Pete.

"I'm going to need a full statement from you and your where-abouts this morning. We're not arresting Mr. Younkin, but he is being detained until we have more information."

Pete's eyes still held a malicious glint, but he nodded sharply.

"Of course. I'm happy to do my civic duty. Now, when do you think we can reopen the truck? Tex would've wanted me to keep going. I owe it to him. To his memory."

"I'm very sorry, but that's not happening today," Ray said, visibly marshaling his patience. "This is a crime scene and we're going to need to go over it carefully. I can't control the rest of the festival, but this area is closed to the public. Unfortunately, Ben and Hannah, that means you, too. I'm sorry, but since you're employed by our prime suspect, I can't allow you to remain here."

I wanted to argue, but Ben nodded and gave Ray a friendly smile.

"Absolutely, Chief. I understand. When do you want to take our statements? We're happy to stick around."

"Let me get the coroner situated and I'll be back, okay?"

"Are you planning on taking off once we give our statements?" I asked once Ray was far enough away that he couldn't hear us. "You heard what Burt said. He wants help. He needs help. I don't think he did it."

Ben's lips curled up in a smile, and he bent closer.

"I know. But I don't want to set Ray's back up. We'll give them their space to investigate, but that doesn't mean we can't interview the other vendors and get a feel for the players. Just because Burt seemed innocent doesn't mean he is. We need more information. That's why I said we'd hang around and that's why he wants us to give our statements right away. Ray's a smart man."

"Ben, Hannah, can I talk to you for a second?"

We turned as one to see Sam jogging towards us. The day was warming quickly, and Canyon Falls was definitely warmer than the climate we were used to at home. Sweat trickled down Sam's face.

"What's up?"

Sam looked around before turning his back in Ray's direction.

"I've got Mr. Younkin waiting in the patrol car, but he's asking to talk to you before they take him to the station. Look, I know it's irregular, but..."

"If you don't think Ray will mind, I'm happy to go talk to him," Ben said, clapping him on the arm.

"If you make it quick, there's no need for him to know. I grew up with Burt's daughter. I've known the man my whole life. I don't think he's a murderer."

"You never know. Sometimes people surprise you. I'll go have a quick chat with him. Let Ray know we'll be right back."

Ben led the way towards the patrol car and I jogged after him, trying to keep up with my much shorter legs. I was puffing and sweating by the time we got to the car. The back window was rolled down, and the bored officer in uniform was sitting in the front seat.

"Ben Walsh," Ben said, nodding to the officer. "He wanted to talk with me."

"Suit yourself, but make it quick. I've gotta get him back to the station. We shouldn't even be doing this."

Burt was seated, his hands between his knees, and the vibrant man seemed to have shrunk into himself since the last time I saw him. Tears streaked down his face and his eyes were full of sorrow as Ben leaned down to talk with him.

"You asked for me?"

"I didn't have time to hire you formally, but I need your help. I didn't do this. I know I'm innocent, but these cops don't know that. It looks bad. I can see that. Pete's always hated me and I wouldn't put it past him to manufacture evidence to put me away for the rest of my life. You've gotta help me find out who killed Tex. I'll pay you whatever you ask."

"I don't think they're going to book you," Ben said, shaking his head. "They've got to have a suspect and unfortunately, you're a very handy one since he was killed with one of your custom barbecue tools. Tell you what. I'll do what I can and once you've been questioned, we'll meet and figure out if you want to go forward with hiring me."

"There's no doubt about that," Burt said, wiping his face with his sleeve. "Tex was a good man. Yeah, I know I was salty about him earlier, but I'd never wished him dead. I want to know who killed him and I'll pay for whatever it takes to make that happen. Tex deserves justice."

"And you don't think our department will do that?" The officer in the front seat spun around, glaring at Burt. "I think you've talked to this guy long enough."

The window rolled up as Ben stepped back with a rueful smile.

"Well, I can't blame him."

We watched as the patrol car swung around and headed out of the fairgrounds. People lined the midway, watching him go, talking amongst themselves. My instincts perked up as I overheard a few snippets of conversation coming from the vendor booth behind us.

"This looks like a good place to ask questions. Do you want to do this together, Detective Walsh, or split up to cover more ground?"

Ben smiled, and his green eyes crinkled at the corners.

"We have a little time. You take this side and I'll start over there. I'm guessing it will be about twenty minutes before Ray tracks us down."

I gave him a cheeky salute before turning on my heel. The booth I was standing in front of was staffed by an older woman and her assistant, and they whispered to each other, looking after the patrol car. The sign above the booth proclaimed it to be Freya's Western Art. So this was the young girl Burt's grandson was seeing. Interesting. I smiled and approached, eager to learn what they had to say.

5

$\mathcal{T}$he owner of the booth had long blonde hair, interspersed with gray, styled in an intricate braid, but her defining feature had to be her crystal-blue eyes, ringed with a darker blue. These eyes narrowed as I approached. The younger woman drifted towards the back of the booth, but her eyes never left my face.

"What's going on? Is it true Tex was murdered? Why was Burt in that patrol car? I don't recognize you, but you sure seem like you know him."

I smiled, hoping to defuse the sharp sting of the suspicion laced, rapid-fire questions she was sending my way. I'd been among the vendors for just a few brief hours, but it was clear they formed a tight-knit family.

"I'm Hannah Murphy. Mr. Younkin hired my boyfriend for some private detective work," I said, pointing towards where Ben was standing at a booth across the way. "Burt's been taken in for questioning on Tex's death. How did you hear about it?"

She thawed a little and tilted her head to the side.

"I'm Freya, and this is Chrissie, my niece. Gerald ran over here a few minutes ago and broke the news. I just don't understand it. Who would want to hurt Tex? He was a big old teddy bear. And why on earth is Burt getting hauled in? He wouldn't hurt a fly."

"That's what we're trying to figure out. The police will be along shortly to ask you some questions, but in the meantime, we're trying to help Burt. We don't know when exactly Tex was killed, but Burt's going to need an alibi, especially after the dustup he had with Tex about the missing ingredients and tools."

"Is it true he was stabbed in the back with one of Burt's skewers?" Chrissie asked, her voice barely audible above the crowd behind me.

She may have been Freya's niece, but she was a mirror image of her aunt. Tall, blonde, and with the same startling eyes.

"It's true. I found the body with Sheila. Oh, speaking of Sheila, she's having a rough time. I don't know if the festival is going to get shut down, but if it isn't, she's going to need some help with her booth. Do you know anyone who could pitch in?"

"Poor Sheila. She's always been a sensitive soul. Of course, we'll help. Chrissie, go on over there and see what she needs."

Chrissie nodded, but it was clear she'd rather stay. She grabbed her purse, but her feet dragged as she left the booth. Freya watched before turning back to me, her eyes keen as they searched my face.

"You think Burt is innocent?"

Something about the way she phrased her question made me pause and my doubts, so recently stamped out, resurfaced again as I remembered the way Burt had looked towards Tex's food truck.

"You know him better than I do. What does your gut tell you?"

She smirked and put her hands on her hips.

"Good one. Deflect and turn it around. What do you do for a living?"

I smiled and shook my head.

"I'm a reporter up in Golden Hills."

"Ah. That makes sense. But back to Burt. I've known him for, oh, it must be nearly a decade since I started my booth here. I don't know if he told you, but most of us are on a circuit all Spring and Summer. I have a regular store, but most of my sales come from these events. It's a great way for artists to get their names out there. He's got a temper, but he's a decent man. If he wasn't, I would've shown his grandson the door as soon as he started sniffing around Chrissie."

"When did you get here this morning?"

"I came early. This is only my second festival of the season, so I like to come and make sure I've got everything set up just the way I want it. I was here probably around eight."

I turned and looked down the midway towards Burt's truck. It was just visible from here.

"And Burt and Tex were already here?"

"Yes ma'am. I spotted Burt setting up as I pulled in. He makes his sauces ahead of time, but everything else is made fresh, so he needs to get the kitchens going pretty quickly. You'd be surprised at how many people want a green chile burger for breakfast."

After spending several years in Colorado, I honestly wasn't that surprised. It may not be a traditional breakfast food, but some people swore by it.

"And did you see him all morning?"

She shrugged and leaned forward, looking at Burt's truck.

"I spotted him off and on, but I've been busy getting everything arranged. I can't swear that he was there the whole time. I know Gerald spent about a half hour here helping me with the heavier things. He's a good boy."

"Can you think of anyone besides Burt who had problems with Tex?"

She looked around before leaning forward, and my radar pinged.

"I don't like to gossip, and I don't think she did anything, but Sheila and Tex were an item a little while back. Things cooled off between them," she said, spreading her hands. "I don't know the details, but there were some pretty hard feelings on her side. From what I've gleaned, Pete played a big role in them breaking things off."

Interesting. Sheila had mentioned nothing about her relationship with Tex. Given that their trucks were side by side, had they parted amicably? Were they still seeing each other quietly? Questions swirled in my head, but Pete and his angry tirade stuck out the most, so I picked that angle.

"Tell me more about Pete. He seemed, well, volatile."

Freya smirked and raised an eyebrow.

"That's a good word for him. He's always been a firebrand. He's the mover and shaker of their business. Tex? He just loved to cook, and he loved to make sure people enjoyed his food. He was an artist in a way, just like me. Except his expression was in sauces and perfectly smoked ribs, not oil paints and canvas. Pete's the business manager."

"Do you think Pete could have killed him? Tex was a big man. Whoever killed him would also need to be pretty sizable, I'd think."

"And kill the golden goose? No, Pete wouldn't shoot himself in the foot that way. In fact, Pete has the most to lose with Tex dying. He's a terrible cook. Without Tex, Pete is nothing."

Maybe that explained Pete's violent reaction to Tex's death. Without the star of the show, the Pit Stop Barbecue would probably close.

"Can you think of anyone else who would hated Tex enough to kill him?"

"I can't. We all loved him. He was a good man. I hope you find out who did it, though. The thought of a murderer creeping around here scares the stuffing out of me," she said, rubbing her arms. "I almost hope the organizers close the festival down, even though I need the revenue."

I dug a card out of my bag and handed it to her.

"If you think of anything, call me. Well, call the police and tell them, too, but I'd sure appreciate a call as well. They'll be coming by to question you. There's no need to mention our little chat, though."

She smiled, her magnificent eyes gleaming.

"I understand. Thanks for looking after Sheila. That was nice of you to want to help her. I don't know how she felt about Tex after they broke up, but it had to hit her hard, finding him like that. Between the rest of us, we'll make sure she's okay. Maybe Vera Bradenton saw something. She's in the next stall over. I'm sorry I couldn't be of more help."

Interesting. Why hadn't Sheila mentioned her involvement with

Tex? I filed that away with other questions I wanted to ask later. I looked around at some of Freya's paintings and wished I had a little more disposable income to afford them.

"Thanks, Freya. It was nice meeting you."

She nodded, and I moved towards the next booth that was jam-packed with western clothing. The woman standing behind the counter stared at me, her face expressionless. Her dark brown hair was styled like a helmet and I seriously doubted it would move if gale force winds blew through the tent.

"T-shirts are two for twenty. Everything else is priced as marked. If you're gonna touch anything, I expect your hands to be clean."

After Freya's warm exchange, it felt like plunging into an ice tub in this tent. Something told me Ben might get further with this woman, but I was here and I needed to make the best of it.

"Good morning. Are you Vera? I just have a few questions for you. I assume you've heard about Tex."

"That's me. If you wanna talk to me, you're gonna have to buy something. Those are the rules. I can't just sit in here gossiping all day. What the other vendors do is their business, not mine. I heard you over there talking to Freya. I don't know how Tex got himself killed, and I don't want to know."

Wow. I'd met some unfriendly people in the course of my work, but this lady took the cake. I kept smiling, though, and walked towards the t-shirt display.

"Of course. I completely understand. Are you on the regular festival circuit?"

"Yep. I do Colorado and South Dakota."

Oh, common ground! I grasped that thread and clung to it like a limpet.

"I'm from South Dakota! Do you do the rally in Sturgis?"

"Most years."

Vera took being taciturn to a whole new level. Deflated, I spotted a rack of baby t-shirts and immediately thought of the cats. One of my missions in life was to dress Razzy up in cute outfits. I'd failed miserably at it so far, but there was always a chance. I zeroed in on a cute baby tee that proclaimed the wearer to be Mama's Lil Cowgirl and grabbed it, repressing the urge to squeal in delight. If Razzy didn't want to wear it, I could give it to my friend Ashley's little girl, Grace. Ashley would think it was a hoot.

"Those are two for twenty, too. May as well get yourself another one."

Well, when she put it like that. I went through the rack and found another cute tee that would definitely go to Grace.

"Here, I'll take these two."

"Fine."

She shuffled behind the counter and stabbed the keys on her calculator with a pointy fingernail.

"That'll be twenty-one-twenty with tax."

I reached for my wallet and dug out some cash while she stuffed the shirts in a tiny bag. If I was going to get anything out of her, I needed to work quickly, especially if someone else wandered in and took her attention away.

"Thank you. Did you notice anything strange this morning? See anyone who didn't belong?"

"I mind my own business, like I said. It's enough work getting this set-up. I don't have time to be gawking at other people."

My shoulders slumped as I took the bag. Maybe the police would have better luck with her. I wondered if she'd make them buy something, too.

"Have a good day," I said, giving her one last look before turning to leave.

"Well, it's better than the day Tex had, I guess. He should've watched his back."

I stopped in my tracks and turned to face her again.

"Why?"

Her face was still expressionless, but if I wasn't mistaken, there was a nasty gleam in her eyes.

"Shouldn't we all watch our backs? You let your guard down and bam, somebody comes up behind you and stabs you in the back."

She turned away, ending the conversation, as someone else

strolled into the tent. I listened as she began her sales pitch before forcing my feet to move. Had she already heard the way he'd died? Was it a coincidence she'd used those exact words? I spotted Ben a few feet away and had to keep from running to his side, chilled by Vera's words. He turned and smiled, and some warmth came back to my soul.

"Any luck?" he asked.

"Well, I found out a few things and got a couple t-shirts," I said, looking back over my shoulder at the clothing stand. "How about you?"

"A few things, but nothing that proves Burt is innocent. Hopefully Ray will share the time of death with us."

"If not, I bet Sam will. He seemed to like Burt. Is there anyone else you want to talk to?"

"I know we planned to eat here, but it looks like everything is getting shut down," Ben said, pointing to where the food vendors were clustered around. "I say let's find Ray, give our statements, and then we head home. We can grab something to eat on the way and run some background checks when we get home."

"Sounds like a plan to me. I'll call Tom and see if he wants me to file a story on it. It's close enough to home. I think it warrants coverage."

I caught Vera staring at us as we reversed direction and headed back to towards the food vendors. I couldn't shake the malevolent feeling that clung to us until we were out of her sight. As soon as I got home, she was going to be the first person I looked up.

We found Ray and Sam behind the barbecue truck, heads bent together. As soon as Ray noticed us, he nodded and patted Sam on the arm before joining us.

"Nasty business. These folks aren't what I expected. You'd think with one of their own being murdered, they'd be in a hurry to shut down their shops and go home."

"I think a lot of them rely on this revenue, Chief," Ben said, looking around the scene. "Find anything interesting back here?"

Ray smirked and took off his hat, scratching at his sparse scalp.

"A few things, but you know I can't share them with you as much as I'd like to. How about you? Find out anything interesting from the vendors you talked to?"

His eyes held a twinkle, letting me know he wasn't all that angry we were sniffing around his turf.

"A couple," I said. "Nothing definitive, though."

"It will be easier if we work together, at least off the books," Ray said. "You're sure you want to keep working for Burt?"

Ben nodded and met the chief's gaze.

"For now. I believe he's innocent, but it would be helpful to know the time of death, if possible. That will definitely weigh on my decision."

"I suppose I can share that intel. I asked the coroner to put a rush on the autopsy. While I've got you, I want to hear from each of you, in your own words, what you saw today. Hannah, you can go first."

I relayed everything I'd noticed while Ben waited. Once I was done, I left Ben to his statement and wandered toward's Sheila's truck, still curious why she'd neglected to tell me about her relationship with Tex. I found her with Chrissie, closing down the truck.

Gerald paced nearby, his face flushed. He brightened when he saw me.

"Miss? It's true? They took my grandpa away?"

He looked like he was close to breaking down, and I had a feeling Chrissie's proximity was the only reason he was holding himself together.

"They're just detaining him to ask some questions. He hasn't been arrested."

"What do I do? I mean, with the food truck. I don't know what to do. They're telling us we need to shut down, but I've never done this on my own before."

His voice cracked, and he flushed, glancing towards Chrissie. She gave him a gentle smile and walked closer.

"It will be okay, Gerry. I'll help, and I know Aunt Freya will lend a hand if we need her. We can just save the food that's already been made and get everything turned off and put away until tomorrow."

I watched his face as she spoke soothingly. Chrissie might be a teenager, but she had a good head on her shoulders. Sheila joined them and wrapped the boy in a hug.

"I'll help, too. You're not alone. None of us really think Burt did it. Your grandpa is a good man."

She herded the young couple towards Burt's truck, but I didn't miss the way she avoided meeting my eyes. Something was going on there, and I needed to find out what it was.

6

I walked into our apartment and between the rapturous greeting of the cats, to just being around our things made me feel like everything was normal again. The morning had felt surreal and somehow twisted from our everyday lives. I scooped Razzy up and snuggled her.

She purred for a moment before twisting in my arms and pinning me with a blue gaze.

"What's wrong? Not that I don't appreciate the cuddles or anything, but you're very unsettled. Ben is too. We felt it when you were on your way home."

I buried my face in her fur and marveled at how sensitive they were. More than once, they'd used those feelings to save our lives. In fact, the last time Ben had gone to Blanco Ridge, I'd only found him thanks to their abilities to tell where we were. I didn't understand how it worked, and honestly? I didn't care. All I knew was that our cats were incredibly special.

Ben stroked my back before bending down to pet Gus and Rudy. He stood back up and smiled at both of us.

"Razzy, Hannah got you something special while we were at the fair. Would you like it now?"

Her beautiful eyes narrowed as she sniffed the air. Gus and Rudy put their fuzzy heads together, and I felt terrible as I realized I hadn't gotten them anything. I passed Razzy over to Ben and dug into my bag. As I pulled out the t-shirt, Her ears went nearly flat.

"No. We've had this conversation before. I don't need clothes. No. No. No."

Rudy let out a sound that resembled a giggle, while Gus huffed out a laugh. Suddenly, they weren't so disappointed that they had been left out. Razzy squiggled in Ben's arms until he gently put her on the couch. She stamped a white mittened paw and shook her head.

"Absolutely not."

"But, Razz, it says your Mama's lil cowgirl! Look how cute this is. And the blue matches your eyes."

Did she thaw a little? Appealing to her vanity usually worked, unless, of course, it had anything to do with a costume. She gave me a long look before sighing, her little kitty shoulders slumping.

"I will wear it for five minutes. You get one picture. One. That's it. I sense this means a lot to you, and far be it from me to deny you anything. I mean, I am just a helpless little cat, subject to the whims of my human. Who am I to choose what I wear?"

I hopped in place, letting her heavy sarcasm wash right over me, and approached her with the tee. Rudy and Gus stared in awe as I slipped it over her little head and gently put her paws through the armholes. If looks could kill, Ben would've been scraping my poor body off the floor as I fluffed her ruff out and arranged it around the neck.

"Happy?"

Even though she was glaring, I could tell she really wanted to see how she looked. She posed gracefully as I pulled out my phone and snapped a picture that would live in infamy, at least in our little family. Once I was done, Rudy and Gus hopped onto the couch.

"You look really pretty, Razzy," Rudy said, ducking his head shyly. "But you always do."

"She's right. The blue matches your eyes. I like it."

I held the phone so she could see herself, and she tilted her head to the side slightly.

"Hmph. Not bad."

She looked mortified as she realized I might take her words as license to buy her more clothes, or heaven forbid, actual costumes, and stammered. Ben finally broke into laughter, and I quickly joined in.

"Oh, Razz. I won't make you wear clothes again. Unless, of course, you want to," I added hopefully.

"I'm getting itchy. Can I take it off now?"

"Of course. I'll wash this and give it to Gracie. Ashley will think it's a hoot."

Razzy shook herself before madly grooming her fur back into its usual position. I folded the little shirt and smoothed out the design. Would we have our own little cowgirl someday? A human one? Maybe I should keep the shirt. I shook off the thought and turned back to the cats.

"Okay, so are you going to tell us what's really going on?" Razzy said, pausing her grooming routine for a moment. "What happened at the fair? We didn't expect you back until later tonight."

"Not that we're complaining. We were just... uh... nothing. Never-mind. What happened at the fair?" Rudy asked.

If cats could blush, I would swear his cheeks would've been stained red. What had they been up to when we were gone? Ben cleared his throat and launched into an abbreviated account of our morning, starting from when we met Burt to interviewing the store owners. By the time he was finished, Razzy was standing upright, lashing her tail.

"I knew it! We can't let you two go anywhere without us. You're constantly tripping over dead bodies. If we'd been there, we could have examined the scene."

"What are we waiting for?" Rudy asked, jumping in the air. "If we go now, the trail might not be cold! We can catch the killer."

"Whoa, guys. Hold your horses. The police have the scene locked down and they're doing their investigation. We can't do anything there."

"You said it's in Chief Weston's jurisdiction, right?" Gus said, his deep voice quiet. "He's a good man. He might be open to our help."

I looked at Ben, but he shook his head.

"I don't know, guys. Since I'm basically working for Burt, it's a conflict of interest. Until Burt's cleared, there's nothing he can share with us. With any luck, Burt will be cleared quickly."

"And that's happened how many times?" Razzy asked. "We've dealt with this before. Every time, the local cops get it wrong and we have to set them straight. We can't let an innocent man hang!"

"Colorado doesn't have the death penalty," Rudy said, glancing at Razzy. "But I get your point."

I bit my lip to keep a laugh from breaking through. He sounded so knowledgeable. Rudy was a born researcher and, thanks to the tablets we'd gotten, he had a way to pursue his quest for more information. Apparently, criminal justice was his new obsession. I couldn't dissuade him. It was better than the alien fixation he'd had a few months ago.

"I was speaking metaphorically," Razzy said, giving him a narrow glare before turning to me. "So, who's your suspect?"

I sat next to her on the couch and shrugged.

"I'm not sure. Whoever it was would have to be pretty strong. Tex was tall and had to weigh at least three hundred pounds. Running him through with a barbecue skewer wouldn't be a simple task."

"So, that nixes the women?"

I thought about the look Vera gave me and shuddered.

"I don't know about that. There are plenty of strong women. We've got some names, so why don't we run some background checks before dinner and see what we can come up with? I think we can do that without making Chief Weston mad."

Razzy nodded and leapt over to the coffee table where my laptop was sitting. She nosed it before looking at me.

"Well, what are waiting for?"

Ben chuckled and pressed a kiss on the top of my head before heading to the kitchen.

"I'll get you some water while you appease the tiny tyrant."

"I am not a tyrant!"

Razzy's eyes blazed in a mixture of horror and indignation, while Rudy and Gus hopped onto the table next to her. I grabbed my laptop and settled down on the couch.

"I need to turn in a piece about the murder, too. Tell you what, guys. I'll do that first and then we can run the vendors afterwards."

Ben reappeared, carrying two glasses of water.

"I can start the search while you're writing," he said, putting the glasses down. "Will that make you guys happy?"

A chorus of yowls answered that question nicely, and all five of us settled down to work. Until I had confirmation that Tex's relatives had been notified, I wouldn't run his name in my initial column. Since the fair wasn't in our county, I'd been lucky to get authorization from Tom to run my piece at all, but so far, it had been a slow weekend and he promised to find a space for it.

I was just wrapping up my piece when Ben sat up straight on the couch.

"What? Did you find something interesting?"

"You said the clothing vendor's name was Bradenton, right?"

"Yep. Vera Bradenton. Why?"

"Well, she must have gone back to her maiden name. Five years ago, her last name was Randolph."

"She was married to Tex?"

"You've got it."

"No way! She didn't say a word! Wouldn't you be surprised that your ex-husband was just murdered a few yards away?"

"Unless she's the one who killed him," Razzy said. "Do you think she could've done it?"

I thought back to my brief interaction with Vera. She wasn't a tall woman, but she was solid. If she'd snuck up behind Tex, would she have had the strength to run a skewer through him? I shook my head.

"I don't know. She seemed like she had a lot of anger simmering under the surface."

"And rage can make people more powerful than you'd imagine," Ben said. "I'll keep looking into her background."

"I wish we knew when Sheila began seeing Tex. I wonder why she said nothing about their relationship? It couldn't have been easy for her to find her ex-lover dead on the ground."

"We need to know more about Tex," Rudy said, his little face solemn. "From what you're saying, he was a man that at least two women wouldn't miss. Why is that?"

Ben stroked Rudy's head and nodded.

"Good point, bud. I've been focusing on the suspects, and not on him."

"I'll search Tex's background," I said, tapping on a few keys to send my article through my newspaper portal. "Keep going with everyone else. I have a feeling we're about to learn a lot more about the fair vendors and what goes on behind closed doors."

Razzy snuggled next to me, her warmth comforting me as I typed Tex's name into my background search tool. To start, I focused on results that would tell me more about his personal life. His criminal record was non-existent, but I found a record of his divorce with Vera and a marriage before that.

"Huh. His first wife's maiden name was Williams. Do you think she's related to Pete?" I asked Ben.

He pulled his eyes away from the screen and shrugged.

"Might be. It's a common name. You could run her quickly and find out. Maybe she had an axe to grind with him, too."

I typed in her full name and waited for the results. The first thing that popped up was her obituary. I clicked the link and began reading.

"Deborah Williams, aged 53, died at Fair Winds Hospice. It lists her surviving relatives as her husband, Tex, and a brother named Peter. It's got to be him, Ben."

"Well, I guess she's not a suspect. Tex and Pete must have been pretty close. I wonder how he felt about Tex remarrying?"

"Hard to say. This is interesting. Remember Curt Wilder? I talked to him while you were talking to Freya."

"The saddle maker?"

"That's him. He's got a few prior arrests for assault. He's as skinny as a rail, but rancher types have that wiry strength that belies their size. He goes on our list, for sure."

I reached for my trusty notebook and began a list of suspects. Even though I relied on my laptop to do the heavy lifting, there was something about writing things down that solidified the facts in my head. Ben added a few more people that he talked to, and by the time I was done, we had a sizable list. Now, we just needed to narrow it down. I had a feeling that would not be as easy as we hoped.

7

*E*ven though I'd wished for a lazy weekend, I couldn't deny the energy sweeping through the kitchen the next morning, even though I hadn't had my coffee yet. Razzy, typically not a morning cat, was bouncing off the walls as I got their breakfasts ready.

"Mama, when are we leaving for the fairgrounds?"

This was the second time in the past ten minutes she'd asked me that question, and I still hadn't figured out a way to tell her I wasn't sure they were coming with us. Even though they were incredibly well behaved, and I usually took her everywhere with me, this time, something was telling me not to take them. I glanced at Ben, hoping for backup.

"In about a half an hour, Razzy," Ben said, shooting me an apologetic look. "We'll get ready while you guys are eating breakfast."

Rudy let out a yowling cheer and did a quick lap around the kitchen, skittering on the slick surface. Gus watched, amusement clear in the tilt of his whiskers. I put their bowls at the table and followed Ben back to our bedroom.

"Are you sure this is a good idea?" I asked before pulling a hoodie over my head, muffling my voice.

"I can't tell them no. They've been looking forward to this ever since we finished our list of suspects. They can't wait to do some sniffing around on their own. We'll keep a good eye on them and make sure they're next to us."

It should have settled my mind, but I still couldn't shake the feeling we were making a mistake. I glanced at my watch and wondered if it was too early to call Anastasia. Would the spirits she seemed in contact with have any advice?

I remembered that when the spirits shared their thoughts, they were often too convoluted to understand in the moment, usually only becoming clear after the fact. No, I'd let her sleep in. It was a Sunday morning, and I was being silly. I nodded to my reflection in the mirror as Ben smiled from across the room.

"Have you decided?"

I smiled back and shrugged.

"You know me. If overthinking was an Olympic event, I'd take gold every single time."

"You always take the gold for me."

He folded me into a hug, and my worries receded to the back of my mind. We'd keep them safe.

"They are very good at finding things people miss. You're right. I don't know why I'm being such a worrywart."

The sound of skittering paws alerted me to Rudy's arrival, and I glanced over just in time to see him sliding past the door.

"Whoops, I overshot," he said, mumbling to himself.

I quickly finished getting ready while Ben went out to round the little heathens up and put them in their carriers. I took one last look at the mirror and nodded again.

"Okay, I'm ready if you're ready."

Razzy let out a cheer and clawed the plush lining of her bag. It had been a few weeks since she'd had a case to sink her claws into and my little sleuth was raring to go. I picked up her bag and followed Ben to the car.

"Who are we going to visit first? I'd like to look at the scene of the crime," she said, once we were on our way.

"If Ray doesn't mind, we'll do that," Ben said, looking at her in the rearview mirror. "Otherwise, I thought we'd see if Burt is around. He hasn't returned my calls, which is odd."

"Do you think Ray ended up charging him?"

Ben glanced at me and shook his head.

"I don't know. If they found evidence that linked him to the murder, they might have. I was hoping Ray would call, but it's been radio silence."

Razzy climbed into my lap and snuggled close, looking out the window.

"You still think he's innocent?"

I stroked her back and thought about it. We'd come up with an impressive list of suspects the night before, but unfortunately, Burt was still at the top. He had a motive, and the murder weapon belonged to him.

"I don't know for sure, baby girl. I hope so. He seems like such a nice man. I can't let that cloud my vision, though."

"Maybe we'll be able to tell. I hope he's around."

"Do you think it was a one-off?" Gus asked.

I turned to look at the big cat, who loved watching old mafia movies and had integrated their lingo into his daily conversations.

"I sure hope so. I would hate to think the other vendors might be in danger."

And with that cheery thought, we quieted as Ben drove. He finally switched on the radio, but we were all too preoccupied with our thoughts to sing along. Even the beautiful morning couldn't dispel the gloom that settled on my shoulders.

"What's the King Valley bridge?"

Rudy's question pierced the silence in the car, and I was glad for the distraction.

"It's a long bridge that cuts across a valley in the Sangre de Cristo mountains. I think at one time it was the longest bridge of its kind. It's a big tourist attraction but I've never been. Ben?"

"Nope, I've seen pictures, though. I'm not a fan of heights, so I've never been tempted. I've heard there are ziplines across and gondola rides."

"That sounds like fun," Razzy said.

"Okay, my little daredevil. Maybe someday we'll take a trip over there. It's a little way from Canyon Falls. I wonder if they'd let us take cats across?"

Ben paled and shook his head.

"I'd have to wait for you. The thought of being suspended over a drop that big just doesn't sound like fun."

He pulled into the fairgrounds and we found a place to park that was closer to the food trucks.

"Okay, guys. Let's get your harnesses on. I want everyone to stick close today. No running off."

Razzy leaned into me, her warmth bringing me reassurance.

"Don't worry. We'll be fine."

Ben led the boys in front of us once everyone was harnessed. It didn't take long for people to take notice of our three large cats walking calmly beside us. Razzy walked confidently, tail held high, looking around like a queen at her loyal subjects.

Ben turned and beamed, enjoying everyone's reaction. I looked around the midway and noticed that it was crammed with people, far more than had been there the day before. It looked like news of the murder had spread. Ben motioned he was continuing on while I stopped at Freya's booth and found Chrissie manning the register. She brightened when she saw Razzy at my feet.

"Oh my goodness, that's a cat!"

The woman she was helping huffed in irritation as Chrissie swept around the counter to kneel in front of Razzy.

"She's adorable. Look at those eyes!"

"Excuse me, I'd like to finish paying."

Chrissie's eyes met mine as her face flushed and she scurried back to finish the translation. The woman sniffed loudly as she passed us.

"People will try to claim service animals for anything these days."

Razzy's eyes filled with indignation as the woman swept past. I scooped her up and held her close.

"Sorry to get you into trouble. Is Freya around?"

"She's down helping Gerry. Did you hear?"

My stomach fell as I shook my head.

"No, what?"

"Burt's been arrested. I guess they found his prints on the skewer, and no one else's. Gerry's devastated. He can't believe his grandpa killed someone," she said, looking around before she lowered her voice. "But I don't think he did it. Burt was in that truck all morning."

"Have you spoken to the police? The chief and the new detective are good men. They'll listen to you."

"I told them what I know, but I might have, well..."

She trailed off and looked down at her scuffed tennis shoes. Razzy gave a little chirp and Chrissie's head came back up as she reached a hand out for Razzy to sniff.

"It's okay. Take your time."

"She's so pretty. What's her name?"

"This is Razzy. I often take her with me when I'm reporting. She's very good with people. Would you like to hold her?"

Chrissie nodded, and I carefully handed Razzy over to her. Razzy tucked her head under the young girl's chin and purred loud enough I could hear her from a few steps away.

"She's so soft. She feels like a stuffed toy."

I waited patiently, knowing that the key to getting someone to talk was to remain quiet. More often than not, they'd fill the silence. It took a few minutes of her lavishing attention on my cat for Chrissie to speak.

"So, I should have told them I saw someone rushing past when I was out back unloading new stock. I didn't see their face, but it was about an hour after we got here yesterday. They were wearing a black hoodie, pulled up around their face. I remembered last night. Now, if I come forward, the police are going to think I'm lying or trying to protect Gerry's grandpa. But I saw someone! I know I did. No one ever goes back behind the trucks, just the owners."

53

"Which direction did they go?" I asked, putting a calming hand on her arm. "It's okay. Sometimes you forget to mention something and only when you're relaxed and comfortable does it come back to your mind."

"They went towards the parking lot. Whoever it was, they were pretty tall."

"Did you tell your aunt?"

Chrissie focused back on Razzy and shook her head.

"No. I didn't know what to do. I'm scared."

"It's okay, Chrissie. You need to let the police know, though. It could be very helpful in finding the killer. Does anyone have any cameras in their trucks or tents?"

"No, not that I know of, anyway. It's tough enough to get power to all of our stuff, and those things are expensive. I know my aunt thought about it, but decided against it. Could you tell the police? They'd listen to you."

"No, but I'll stand with you when you talk to them, okay? Let me give Ray a call and see if he's nearby."

She tightened her hold on Razzy, who purred louder and gave Chrissie a raspy lick on the cheek. The girl giggled as she crinkled her nose.

"Ouch. It's like sandpaper."

I dialed Ray's number and was surprised when he picked up on the first ring.

"Hannah, what's up? I've been meaning to call Ben, but I've been tied up."

"Are you near the fairgrounds? I've got some interesting information for you."

"I'm already on my way. I can be there in five. Where are you?"

"Freya's Western Art. It's close to the food truck section."

"Alrighty. I'm assuming you already heard?"

"We did. Chief, I don't think..."

"I know, Hannah. But we have protocol. If it helps, Burt's being well cared for. I got the judge to agree to an emergency hearing. We're waiting on the coroner, so the hearing might not even be necessary. Talk with you soon."

He ended the call. I stared at my phone's screen for a moment before sliding it into my pocket.

"He'll be here in a few minutes. You're doing the right thing, Chrissie."

She nodded, but still looked like she'd rather be getting a root canal. Another woman entered the tent and Chrissie gave Razzy back before scurrying over to help. I walked a little outside of the tent, still watching Chrissie in the off chance she bolted.

"What do you think?"

Razzy nestled close and spoke so softly I could barely hear her.

"I think she's telling the truth. Who do you think it was?"

"Well, Burt's not the tallest guy out there, so it might help remove him from the suspect list. I wonder if anyone else noticed him?"

"Do the fairgrounds have security? Maybe there are cameras elsewhere that would back her story up."

I looked up and around, but saw no sign of any cameras. She had a point, though. There would have to be some sort of security system, right?

"We'll check it out. I should text Ben and let him know what's going on."

"I'm more than happy to be an emotional support cat for Chrissie again, while she talks to the police. She's got a good heart."

I stroked Razzy's head before letting Ben know what was keeping us. With any luck, he could join us before Ray showed up. The woman Chrissie was helping said something I couldn't hear before walking away, empty-handed.

"Wasn't interested?" I asked Chrissie as she joined me, twisting her hands together.

"Said she might be back. I've learned that means no. I don't know if I can do this."

"You'll be fine, Chrissie. Just take a deep breath. You can hold Razzy again if that will help."

She nodded, and I passed Razzy back over just in time to spot Ray walking towards us. He tipped his cowboy hat at the people he passed. I patted Chrissie's back as she tensed up, looking like she wanted to bolt. Before she could move, Ray was in front of us, and she burst into tears. He looked at me in alarm as she sobbed.

"Now, I know I'm an ugly old cuss, but I don't think I ever made anyone cry just to look at me," he said, taking off his hat and tucking it under his arm. "What's this about, Chrissie?"

She held Razzy tightly as she hiccuped her way through the story. Her pretty blue eyes shone with tears as she finished, and she looked completely wrung out.

"Am I gonna go to jail? I'm sorry I said nothing yesterday."

"No, sweetheart, you're not. I appreciate you having the guts to say something. I'll definitely look into what you saw and see if anyone else noticed him. You think it was a man?"

She nodded, but didn't look completely certain.

"I think so. Freya and I are pretty tall, and whoever it was, was bigger than we are."

Ray nodded slowly and turned as Ben joined us, cats in tow. Ray's wrinkled face broke into a smile as he spotted Rudy and Gus.

"Well, isn't this something else? I remember these guys. It's good to see you."

He crouched down as his knees popped and held out a hand in greeting to the cats. Razzy wiggled in Chrissie's arm and the girl passed her to me quickly.

"Thanks. I was scared I was going to drop her."

Razzy joined in greeting the Chief and I looked over at Ben, surprised at the look on his face. He barely smiled at Ray and he kept looking back over his shoulder the way they'd come. What had happened? I edged closer and tugged on his arm.

"What's wrong?"

"The boys had little chance to snoop around by Tex's truck. Pete showed up and made some nasty comments about cats. I know he's grieving, but I don't like that man. There's something wrong with him. Don't let these guys out of our sight. I think your bad feeling was spot-on."

My stomach twisted painfully. What had Pete said? Was he really grieving, or was he a murderer? All I wanted to do was go check it out myself, but I'd have to wait. I turned back to Chrissie and listened as she described what she'd told me. Ray's face was hard to read, but at least he was listening. I heard a woman's voice and spotted Freya, who resembled a Valkyrie as she stormed towards her shop, face flushed with anger.

8

*C*hrissie trailed off as her aunt came flying into the tent, eyes flashing. Ray tipped his hat but kept the mild look on his face as Freya shouted.

"Why are you interviewing my niece without my permission? She's a minor!"

"Now, Freya, it's okay," Ray said. "She's just telling me about something she saw yesterday that might pertain to Tex's death. I'm not asking her questions, I'm just letting her talk."

Freya's startling blue eyes narrowed, and I nearly took a step back from the sheer force of her anger. She'd seemed so nice the day before. This was definitely a new side to her.

"What are you talking about?"

Chrissie blushed and looked at the ground before mumbling.

"I saw someone behind the trucks yesterday morning. Remember, I was back there unloading the new stock. Oh, that's right. You left, and it was just me. Whoever it was, they were acting suspiciously, and I remembered it last night. I'm sorry I said nothing, Auntie. But I thought it would look weird that I forgot to mention it yesterday when we were being interviewed. Hannah told me I should say something and Ray just got here."

Freya turned towards me and any friendly feelings she might have had for me the prior day were obviously long gone.

"Oh, she did, did she? Well, Hannah, you're not Chrissie's guardian. I am. And I didn't agree that she would be interviewed, questioned, or talk to the police. I will put in a complaint, Ray. You can guarantee that!"

Ray held up a hand and shook his head.

"Now, Freya. There's no need to get all fired up. If Chrissie saw something, it's very important. If Burt's innocent, we need to discover who was back here. It might have been the murderer."

"And that murderer may find out Chrissie's been blabbing to the police and then they'll come after her. I can't believe you'd do something like this," she said, grabbing Chrissie's arm. "Why didn't you say anything to me?"

I motioned for Ben to step back with me and watched as Chrissie shot me a mournful look. I saw Freya in a different light as she argued with the chief of police. She was a tall, powerful woman.

"Let's walk. I'm going to carry Razzy," I said, scooping her up. "Is there somewhere we can go where no one can hear us? Quite a crowd has gathered here."

Ben nodded and held his arms out for the cats. He'd been working on training them to leap into his arms, and it worked like a charm. Rudy was first vaulting easily into the air and clambering up on Ben's shoulders. Gus followed and flowed upward, landing neatly in Ben's outstretched arms.

"Let's go over there," Ben said, nodding towards a patch between the tents and food trucks. "No one's over there and everyone's focused on what's happening here."

I noticed we were between Vera's tent and another food vendor. Vera shot me an unfriendly look as we passed, but I quickly averted my eyes. We certainly weren't winning hearts and minds at this place. I breathed a sigh of relief as we came to a stop and let Razzy down on the grass.

"Wow. I didn't think Freya had it in her. Now, what happened with Tex?"

"You first. What was all that about?"

I quickly relayed what Chrissie saw the day before and realized we were in the perfect spot to see behind the tents. I walked a little further and pointed out the back of Freya's tent.

"Chrissie must have been standing right there. So, let's say whoever she saw killed Tex. They would've had a straight shot from back there," I said, pointing towards Tex's truck. "Towards the parking lot. It could literally be anyone. Unfortunately, she never saw his face."

"Or her face," Ben said, frowning. "It could be a woman. Given what we've learned about Tex's background, it's entirely possible it wasn't a man."

"Or it's Pete. What did he say about the cats?"

Ben's face flushed, and his green eyes went hard.

"He said if he saw them around his stuff again, he'd grab his shotgun."

"He called us vermin, Ma," Rudy said, his blue eyes sad. "We're not dirty mice. I work very hard to stay clean. We all do."

Razzy's eyes narrowed, and she sniffed before shooting a dirty look back towards the food trucks.

"Some people are just awful human beings. That settles it. I think Pete is the killer. It's always the cat hater."

I knelt to stroke her head and wished she was right. It would certainly make the investigation easier. However, I couldn't forget Freya's comments about Pete. Without Tex, he was nothing. But did he realize that? I needed to talk with him, but I'd have to figure out a way to do it without the cats.

"I'm sorry babies. Did you three find out anything else interesting?"

"We didn't have time," Gus said, shifting in Ben's arms. "I was on a scent when that man came out and started yelling. I wish we could go back there."

A plan formed in my mind as I began thinking out loud.

"What if I ask Pete for an interview and get him to come away from the food truck? If what people are saying is true, he's going to be interested in publicity to keep the food truck going. Then, when I've got him away from there, Ben, you can take all three cats over and they'll have time to investigate. I can text as soon as Pete leaves, so you'll have plenty of time to get away."

Ben nodded, but the serious look never left his eyes.

"It could work, but I don't know if I'm comfortable with you being alone with Pete. He's a violent man with a terrible temper."

"I'll keep it as light as possible. He really doesn't have a motive, so I don't think I'll be in too much danger. I'll go talk to him right now," I said, passing Razzy's lead over to Ben. "Once you see us walk by, head back behind here."

Rudy chirped and leaned so far off Ben's shoulder I thought he'd fall, as he gave me a head bump.

"Thanks, Ma! We won't let you down. I'm sure we'll find something important back there."

Razzy gave me a slow blink as Gus shifted in Ben's arms again.

"Be careful, lady. I don't like that man."

I ruffled his fur and winked at him.

"I will. Take good care of these three."

He nodded as I stood on my tiptoes to kiss Ben's cheek and headed back onto the midway. The other food trucks, including Burt's, were busy, with lines of people stretching outside. Only a few people were clustered around the Pit Stop, and they didn't look happy. As I got closer, a couple passed, talking loudly.

"That's just not good. Did you taste the sauce? It was so bitter. I thought it would be better with all the awards they've won."

"Isn't the owner the one who got murdered? I thought I heard something on the news about it this morning. If he was, maybe someone killed him over his terrible cooking."

The man laughed loudly at his own joke, and the woman with him tittered as they walked on. I stopped at the counter and saw Pete, staring at the ingredients in front of him, muttering.

"Mr. Williams?"

His head snapped up, and he gave me an unfriendly look.

"You. I remember you. You're the one who found Tex. I wanna talk to you."

He undid the apron around his sizable waist and wadded it up with powerful hands. Suddenly, I doubted if this was a smart idea. But I'd gotten this far, and I needed to get him away from the truck.

"That's serendipitous, because I want to talk with you, too. I'm a reporter for the Golden Hills Post, and I'd like to do a story about Tex's life. Do you have a few minutes? Maybe we can go somewhere quieter and talk."

"This place is as silent as a grave," he said with a snort. "But I gotta get away from here. There's a cafe at the entrance to the fairgrounds. No one knows me well there."

He banged open the folding counter and hopped down as the food truck bucked wildly in place from the change in weight distribution. He didn't look back as he plowed ahead, straight through the center of the midway. I scurried to catch up with him, glancing at Ben and the cats as I walked. I just had time to shoot them a thumbs up before Pete turned back.

"You coming?"

"Yes, Mr. Williams."

By the time we left the main area with the vendors, I was panting with the effort of keeping up with the much taller man. As usual, I swore I was going to run to stay in shape. Tomorrow. Yep, that's when I'd start my new fitness quest. Yeah, I don't believe me either.

Sweat was dripping unpleasantly down my back as we walked up to the tiny cafe that was attached to the fairgrounds. The interior was dingy, painted in varying shades of gray, and the women behind the counter wore a sore expression.

"We're closing in fifteen minutes. What do you want?"

Pete ordered a coffee, and I asked for a bottle of water. Both got slammed down on the counter, and Pete's coffee slopped over the edge, adding yet another stain on the counter's surface.

"Ten bucks."

My eyebrows went up, but I dutifully handed over a ten-dollar bill, which got slammed into the register. Okay then.

I followed Pete back outside and joined him at a rickety table. The chair I'd picked was shorter on one side and I nearly tipped backward. It was a good thing I hadn't taken the lid off my water bottle yet, or I'd have splashed it all over myself.

Pete didn't notice. He was too busy staring back the way we'd come, his expression twisted with a bundle of emotions. I took a few moments to study him. He wasn't a bad-looking man, but he gave the impression of someone who wasn't concerned with maintaining his appearance. His hair was overgrown, brushing over his ears, and his beard stubble was patchy, threaded liberally through with gray. He was overweight, but looked like he'd been muscular in his youth.

"I've heard about you. Read your articles in the Post. You seem to be good at catching murderers."

I twisted open the bottle and took a sip before answering.

"A few. This isn't my turf, though. Are you from the area?"

"Born and raised," he said, taking a slurping drink of his coffee. "Shouldn't you be asking about Tex? I thought that's who the article was going to be about."

He took another drink, his face twisting into a horrible scowl as he swallowed the vile-looking brew. It made the coffee in the newsroom look delicious, and that wasn't saying much.

"How long did you know Tex?"

He let out a sigh and continued staring back towards the food trucks.

"Been a long time. He married my sister. She passed a few years ago. Cancer. I used to work for the mine. Lost my job when it closed down. Tex took me in and gave me a job. He was a good man. He didn't deserve to die like that."

I saw an opportunity and leapt at it.

"Who do you think did it?"

"You know, in the heat of the moment, it seemed obvious it was Burt. They've always been rivals, but lately it's turned nasty. The more I think about it, though, I don't think he did it. I think it was that shrew."

He glanced at me before risking another drink of coffee.

"Vera?"

"I see you've done your research. Did you know he married her eight months after my sister died? She was barely cold, and he took up with that rank woman. I'll never understand what he saw in her. Tex was the easiest going guy you'd ever meet. My sister was the same way. I don't know what possessed him. They didn't last long, though. Maybe two years and she filed for divorce. Took most of his money."

"And you helped him make it back?"

Pete's eyes shone as he nodded.

"I'd never tried marketing before. Tex told me I'd be ideal. He said I was a smooth talker who could sell ice to Alaskans. And you know what? He was right. I've got a gift. I helped change the menus and got us some publicity. I'm all thumbs with cooking, but I've got the gift of gab. That's what my momma always said, anyway. Turns out she was right."

I kept him talking, reminiscing about his days working with Tex. By the time he was done, I had more than enough material to write a solid human interest piece on Tex, but I wasn't that much further along with figuring out who killed him.

"Tell me more about Vera and why you think she did it. It would have taken a lot of strength to... well, it wouldn't have been easy."

"Oh, don't let her size fool you. I swear she's powered by sheer spite. I never asked him, but I'll bet you dollars to donuts he forgot to change his life insurance policy and I bet you she gets the complete kit and kaboodle. He promised me the food truck, and that was enough for me. Now I don't know what I'll do it with, though."

I blinked. I'd never thought about that. Greed, lust, and wrath were more than just the deadly sins. They were often the most powerful motives for murder.

"Have you told Ray this?"

"Yes, ma'am. We'll see."

"What about the other women in his life?"

"Sheila?" he asked with a snort. "That was just a casual thing, but I don't think she saw it that way. I told him it was a bad idea. I mean, he already had to work close to Vera. Why did he have to take up with

Sheila? But he never listened. I guess he was a romantic at heart. He never got out much, never liked to go to the bars. The only time he left his house was to come to these events."

"Would you say the vendors are a tight-knit community?"

"I'd say they're more dysfunctional than tight-knit. Oh, sure, everyone lends a helping hand, but there's this weird thread of competition in there, too. Take Burt. He's not a bad guy, but he gets crazy when there's a prize involved."

"Are you going to keep the food truck going?"

"Shoot, I don't know what to do. I ain't got much and my skills in the kitchen are plumb awful. I'd have to hire a cook, and I don't know if that's the right move to make. Part of me wants to do it, in Tex's memory, but I don't know if I can."

His enormous shoulders slumped, and he drained the rest of his coffee, crushing the paper cup in his hairy hand.

"I'd better get back to it. Such as it is. I appreciate you writing a piece on Tex. He would've gotten a kick out of seeing his name in print. He always saved his press mentions in a little scrapbook."

"Do you have that? I'd like to see it."

"I think it's somewhere in his things in the office. I'll see if I can find that. Maybe you can use it for your column."

"Thank you."

I twisted the lid back onto my half-empty bottle and shoved it into my bag. This hadn't gone the way I'd expected, but I'd learned more about the vendors. I pushed back my chair as Pete thanked me for the coffee and headed back on his own, shoulder rounded.

I texted Ben to warn him about Pete's return, and followed, lost in thought. How could I find out more about Tex's will and life insurance? I knew Ray would dig that up, but this case intrigued me. I was more convinced than ever that Burt was innocent, but the only problem was, I didn't know who killed Tex. I sighed and picked up the pace. With any luck, maybe Ben and the cats discovered a bombshell that would blow the case wide open.

9

*T*he midway was much busier as I wandered back, still lost in my own thoughts. Someone bumped my shoulder as they walked past, but I didn't bother to turn around to see who it was. I looked ahead and spotted Ben with our three cats at his feet and Ray and Sam Trotter by his side. Worry that he'd gotten in trouble quickened my steps. I came to a stop in front of Vera's tent and noticed she was staring.

Ben smiled, his green eyes crinkling in the corners, and I relaxed a little.

"These cats of yours put police dogs to shame," Sam said, shaking his head. "I've seen nothing like it. They're incredible."

All three cats fluffed up their chests, sitting proudly. I crouched down to pet each one as Ray filled me in on their big find.

"It was the craziest thing I've ever seen," Ray said, taking off his cowboy hat to scratch at his scalp. "They're better than bloodhounds. They found an earring and a scrap of cloth. Our boys went over everything yesterday, but obviously they missed a few things."

I stood back up and smiled at the chief, pride radiating out of my every pore.

"Thanks, Ray. I hope Freya wasn't too mad at you."

He glanced towards Freya's booth and shrugged.

"I've never known her to be like that, but I see her point. Once she understood I wasn't interrogating Chrissie, she calmed down."

I looked around for the young teenager, but didn't see her.

"Where did Chrissie go?"

"She's over there, helping Gerry," Ben said, nodding in that direction. "I'm not sure it's making Gerry more productive, though. That poor kid keeps blushing and dropping everything."

I smiled at the thought of adolescent love before my mind went back to the evidence they'd found.

"Do you think you can get a print off the earring?"

Sam looked at the bag and shook his head slowly.

"It's pretty small, but the lab guy is talented. If anyone can find a partial, it's him. We collected everyone's prints yesterday as a precaution. Oh, we let Burt go. The time of death put him in the clear."

I perked up and glanced over at Ben.

"Really?"

"He was killed within about a half hour of you finding him," Ben said. "Burt was with us and before that, he was seen in his truck by everyone else. Whoever did it wore gloves. The only prints on the tool were Burt and Tex's."

"So, Tex is the one who stole Burt's tools?"

Ben scrubbed at the back of his hair and shrugged.

"It sure looks that way. Unfortunately, we'll never know if it was a harmless prank or not. The whole thing is sad."

"So, now that your client's in the clear, you two will probably clear out, huh?" Ray asked, his eyes twinkling.

I glanced at Ben and bit my lip. We had little reason to stick around. The mystery of who had stolen Burt's tools and, likely, his recipe and ingredients was solved. He was no longer under suspicion of murder, so that meant we had no concrete reason to be here. But I wasn't ready to walk away. I was too invested.

"Um, well..."

Ray laughed and shook his head.

"I figured as much. The two of you are much too stubborn to keep your noses out of things. I don't mind the help, especially with discovering important evidence. But this is still a Blanco Ridge case. Officially..."

"We understand," Ben said, wrapping an arm around me. "We might hang around for the rest of the day and see what else we can find out. I mean, we're already here, and it was a long drive."

Sam laughed, his white teeth flashing in the sun.

"When you put it like that..."

"There is one thing..." I said, tilting my head as I looked at Ray. "Pete mentioned he thought Vera might have done it. He wasn't sure if Tex had ever removed her from his life insurance policy. In fact, he might not have updated his will."

Ray's friendly look shuttered a smidge as he hooked his thumbs through his belt loops.

"We're looking into all avenues, and I appreciate the tip. We're waiting to hear from Tex's lawyer."

He didn't mention that he'd let us know what he found out and the wind went out of my sails a little. I scooped up Razzy and glanced towards Sheila's food truck. It wasn't quite lunchtime, and she was standing behind her counter, wearing an odd expression.

"I'd like to check on Sheila, Ben. Want to come with?"

He nodded, and we said our goodbyes to Ray and Sam before walking towards Sheila's truck. I spotted Chrissie and Gerry at the Green Chile Experience, and they were busy. It was nice of her to help him out. She turned, catching my eyes, and shot me a shy smile.

Unfortunately, Sheila's welcome wasn't nearly as warm as it had been the day before.

"I'm sorry, but I'm allergic to cats and I can't risk having their hair contaminate my food," Sheila said, holding up a hand to cover her nose and mouth.

Ben took Razzy from me and nodded at Sheila.

"No problem, I'll take them away. Hannah, we'll be back over there, okay?"

I nodded and turned back to Sheila. Was I mistaken, or was that a flash of relief in her eyes? Was she truly allergic to cats or did she not want to be around Ben? Interesting.

"How are you holding up?" I asked, searching her face for her reaction.

"What? Oh, fine. Busy."

I looked around the empty food truck before turning back to her.

"Why didn't you tell me you and Tex used to be an item?"

Her mouth fell open, and she blinked several times, surprised. I wasn't sure what made me ask her flat out, but I couldn't take it back now. Instead, I waited for her response.

"Oh. I didn't think it was that important. I mean, it was in the past. We were over. It wasn't a big thing."

Her eyes told a completely different story. They said it was an enormous thing indeed, and that she wasn't over Tex. At all.

"That had to be very traumatic, finding him the way we did. Are you sure you're okay? If you need to talk to anyone, I'm here, or I can recommend someone who could help."

"A shrink?" she asked with a snort. "No, thank you. I don't go in for that mumbo-jumbo. I'm fine. It was startling to find a body, but I haven't really thought about it since."

She was lying, but why? Alarm bells started clanging in my head as she looked around, her movements jerky.

"What was your man doing with those cats back there? I saw them. It looked like they were sniffing around. It's not natural, you know. Seeing cats on leashes like dogs. They belong at home, curled up on the couch."

"You'd be surprised at how adventurous some cats are," I said with a gentle smile. "We lucked out with three who enjoy the great outdoors. Some cats don't, and that's perfectly fine. Each one is their own individual. We make sure they're happy."

"Still weird. What were they doing?"

She picked the dishcloth she was holding with her fingernails, still not meeting my eyes. I wasn't sure why, but something told me I shouldn't reveal what they found. Her ears were pierced, but she wasn't wearing earrings. Had she worn any the day before?

"Oh, I'm sure they were just sniffing around. Cats have very good noses. In fact, they're better than dogs at distinguishing distinct scents."

"Is that a fact? Huh. Well, I need to get back to work," she said, swiping the rag around the spotless counter.

"Is everything okay, Sheila?"

She seemed disappointed that I wouldn't take the hint, but she hadn't banked on how stubborn I could be.

"Yes. I'm sorry. I'm all discombobulated. At first, I thought we were safe when they arrested Burt. I mean, it's terrible that he killed Tex, but now they've let him out. Is he really innocent?"

Her eyes finally met mine, and I didn't like the expression hidden in their depths.

"It looks that way."

"Well, that means the murderer is still out there. It could be anyone," she said, glancing over at the surrounding booths and trucks. "It's not safe. What if one of us is next?"

Did she know something? She was acting so erratically that was the only thing that made sense. I stepped closer and patted her arm, noticing that she shrank away from my contact.

"I got little chance to talk to you yesterday, but did you see anything? Anyone? Someone mentioned seeing a man wearing a dark hoodie behind the food trucks in the morning yesterday."

"Really? Who was it?"

"I don't know. I know the police are looking into it, though. Did you notice anything out of the ordinary?"

For a split second, I thought she was going to tell me the truth, but something kept her lips sealed. She shook her head.

"No. Now, I'm sorry, but I really need to get back to work. If you'll excuse me?"

I stood there for a moment more, hoping she'd crack, but she turned her back to me and began rummaging through the bins where she kept the toppings for the potatoes, ignoring me. I heaved a sigh and walked down the steps, remembering how I'd been surprised by Burt the day before. A chill worked down my spine, and I stood there, looking around.

I walked down the middle of the two trucks. Sheila's truck didn't have a back door, but it was clear from the way the grass was flattened that she walked around back here quite a bit. There was a trash bin behind her van, and it was pretty full. Had she spotted someone and was now too scared to come forward, or was she the one who'd killed Tex?

I tossed around the idea, thinking back to how she'd reacted yesterday when we found Tex. Had her shock been honest? She wasn't tall, but she might be stronger than she looked. Rage made people powerful. Had Tex known the person who'd killed him? If he'd turned his back on someone he trusted, it would have given them the opening to stab him through with a skewer. I shuddered as memories of his lifeless body came back.

He must have died instantly, his heart pierced by the skewer, but were the odds of someone landing a strike that lucky? So many things just didn't add up. I kicked at the dirt and went back to find Ben. My stomach rumbled, reminding me that lunch time was near. Maybe some food would help. I walked back into the midway, now even more crowded, and looked for him. One of the great things about dating a man as tall as Ben was it was easy to find him, even in a crowd.

I turned to my left and saw him walking towards me, Rudy clinging to his shoulders, tail puffed out, and Gus in his arms. Ben's face was drawn and suddenly, my stomach shriveled into a ball, all thoughts of hunger long gone. Something was wrong. Ben never looked like that.

I started walking towards him, nearly tripping over my own feet in my haste. He closed the distance and looked at me, his eyes misty with tears. I grabbed his arm as I looked around for Razzy. Where was she?

"Hannah, I'm so sorry. I don't know how..."

"Where's Razzy?"

"She's gone," he said. "She was with us, on her lead, and the next thing I knew, she was gone."

He held up Razzy's colorful lead, and I gasped as I realized it had been cut clean through, right above where the hasp that hooked onto her harness should be.

"No. No. She can't be gone."

My world tilted, and I felt like I was going to be sick. Where was my little Razzy girl? Had someone taken her? Rudy let out a mournful, low cry, and tears streamed down my face. This could not be happening.

10

*E*ver since Razzy had come into my life, she'd been the puzzle piece that brought everything together. She'd been there through it all, and ever since I gained the ability to understand her, our relationship had strengthened even more. She was more than just a treasured companion. She was my best friend. My legs gave out, and I sunk down into the center of the midway, uncaring that I was making a scene.

Ben knelt next to me, his hand under my arm, and helped me to my feet, pulling me close against him, sandwiching Gus between us.

"We'll find her, lady. Don't worry. I won't sleep until she's back."

I absentmindedly reached for his fuzzy head and looked into Ben's green eyes. Eyes that were full of sadness and loss.

"I'm... I'm so sorry, Hannah. I don't know what happened. But Gus is right. We'll find her. Someone had to have taken her, but you know our Razzy girl. She'll fight to get back to you."

It was like someone pressed play, and the sights and sounds of the crowded fair started up again with a lurch. He was right. No one was going to keep Razzy and me apart. If I had to tear apart the fairgrounds, piece by piece, I was going to find my cat. I took a deep breath and stepped back.

"Okay. Is Ray still around? We're going to need his help. I want this whole place searched."

"I'll call him. Even if he left, he won't be far. I'll show you where we were standing when it happened."

I followed, nearly flying as my heart pounded in my chest. Razzy was a beautiful cat. I could see someone wanting her for her looks alone. A thought blazed to life.

"Does this fair have a 4H show or anything? Did you mention that?"

Ben came to a stop, puzzled and tilted his head.

"Probably. Why?"

Excitement coursed through me and I looked around at all the vendors lined up.

"Maybe someone took her to win the pet show. When I was a kid, I had a lamb I raised to compete in the show. I didn't win, but I had a lot of fun. There were a bunch of different classes. Maybe whoever took her didn't mean any harm, but thought they could win with her."

Rudy leaned closer, his whiskers tickling my face.

"I don't think she'd stand for that. Um... You know how she is," he said, quickly backtracking when he saw the look on my face. "But it's a good idea, Ma. Let's go check."

It was the only idea I had. The only one that meant she would still be here on the grounds and not riding away in someone's car, to disappear forever. I clung to it with every fiber of my being.

Ben nodded slowly and pointed up towards the fairground building, where I'd had coffee with Pete.

"It's up there. Let's go. I'll call Ray while we walk."

I strode ahead, leading the way for the first time, powered by the fear of losing my cat. I turned to see Ben trying to untangle himself from people who'd noticed Rudy riding on his shoulders. The young cat was puffed up, clearly uncomfortable. I walked back quickly and held my arms out to him.

Rudy cleared the distance with one massive leap, and nearly took me with him as he clung to my shirt. He'd definitely gotten bigger and his weight was solid against my chest.

"Sorry, Ma. I just don't like it when people prod and poke at me. So rude!"

I smoothed his ruffled fur, nodded at the curious onlookers, and began walking again. Sam Trotter came into view, his face creased into a pleasant smile.

"Hannah, what's wrong? You look upset."

"I've got to keep going, Sam. Someone stole Razzy, and we're trying to find her."

He put a hand on my arm, forcing me to halt. His brow furrowed. "What?"

Ben caught up and quickly filled Sam in on what happened, showing him the cut lead. Sam frowned as he examined it.

"Whoever cut this used a sharp knife. You think it might have been a kid? I don't know..."

I whimpered and Ben shifted Gus up to his shoulder to free up an arm to wrap around me.

"I know it's a long shot, Sam, but it's all we've got. I've already looked around the area where I was standing. She wasn't there."

"Well, I'll go with you. Have you called Ray?"

"I did. It went to voicemail."

"He was taking the evidence back to the shop to get it analyzed. He's probably out of pocket."

"Can we make sure no one leaves the grounds?" I asked, hope flaring again. "Lock it down so no one can leave until we search their vehicles?"

Sam and Ben exchanged a glance, but I refused to let myself feel like a crazy cat lady.

"That would be very difficult, but I can try my best," Sam said, shifting his weight back and forth.

"We've got to do something. I can't stand by and just let someone take her. If she's not at the show, she could literally be anywhere by now."

I turned on my heel and began walking as fast as I could towards the fairgrounds, uncaring that people were stopping to stare at me. A worried growl rumbled deep in Rudy's chest.

I walked into the low slung building and didn't care that the smell of many confined large animals smacked me right in the face. I turned, trying to get my bearings, and spotted a woman holding a clipboard. I zeroed in on her.

"Hi, excuse me, are you with 4H?"

"Yes, ma'am. Do you have a child competing?"

"No, but I was wondering if you have a small animal show scheduled for today?"

She shot me a look that clearly showed she was worried about my mental stability, particularly given that Rudy was standing on my shoulders, staring at her, too.

"Oh. Yeess... Later on today, actually. They're getting set-up over there, but ma'am, you can't just..."

Whatever she was saying got lost as I hustled towards the direction she'd showed. Rudy clung onto my shoulder, his claws gripping into my skin.

"Sorry, Ma. I almost slipped."

"Sorry, bud," I said, slowing down a touch.

He purred and gave me a head butt before gripping again as I sped back up once the stage came into view. A bunch of young kids were clustered around, talking and staring at their phones.

"Excuse me. Where do they keep the animals before the competition?"

A young kid with a buzz cut tore his eyes away from his phone and goggled up at Rudy.

"Over there. That's a cool cat. What's his name?"

"Rudy. Thanks. I appreciate the help."

I kept going and walked behind a curtain, revealing an area filled with cages and more children. My heart nearly leapt out of my chest when I spotted the dark brown back of a long-haired cat.

"Razzy?"

The cat in question pivoted in her cage, but my heart sank as I realized it wasn't her. The cat in question had beautiful blue eyes that darted up towards Rudy.

"Sorry, my name's Jasmine."

Rudy came tumbling down into my arms, sniffing at the cat through the cage.

"Jasmine, have you seen another Ragdoll cat here?"

Her eyes widened comically as she looked between me and Rudy.

"She can understand me? I'm sorry, that's rude of me to keep talking to him when obviously you understand me. You'll have to forgive my manners, but you see, I've never been in this situation before."

The other cats in the neighboring cages blinked with interest as they listened in.

"Jasmine, are you for real? Hey, can you understand me, too?"

I turned to look at a beautiful male brindled tabby and nodded sharply.

"I can. I'm so sorry to be rude, but we're desperate. My cat was stolen and I'm worried someone took her to compete in your show. She looks a lot like Rudy, but her blaze only goes partway down her face."

Ben showed up, his face red, and nudged me with an elbow.

"Everyone is staring. We'd better work fast. Any luck?"

"Sorry, there's no one named Razzy here," Jasmine said, blinking at Gus in appreciation. "But both of you boys should be in the show. No offense Eddie, but I think this one would have it in the bag."

The brindled tabby flattened his ears and turned away, sulking. I scanned the cages, confirming Jasmine's observations, and turned to Ben, tears welling in my eyes.

"She's not here."

"We knew it was a long shot. It was definitely worth checking. Let's get out of here."

A young girl came forward, her little face sharp with curiosity.

"Are you Selena's parents? I know she was waiting for them to bring her cat. But I don't think I've ever seen you before."

"No, sweetheart. We're looking for a lost cat. She looks a lot like this one," I said, holding Rudy up. "Have you seen her?"

She reached forward to pet Rudy, and he allowed it, bumping her little hand with his head gently.

"No, but he's real pretty. I don't have a cat, but I have a sheep. Do you want to see him? His name's Peter."

I couldn't help but smile at this tiny girl with her blonde pigtails. Ben knelt down, and she reached for Gus, stroking his tufted ears gently.

"Whoa. He's a big cat."

"He is. We're kind of tied up now, but if you see the cat we're looking for, can you come find us?"

"Sure," she said. "You have pretty eyes."

Ben smiled and for a split second, I could see the dad he would be if we ever had kids. That thought led to another wrenching pain in my heart as I remembered how worried Razzy had been that Ben and I would have kids and not want the cats anymore. We had to find her.

"If we find our cat, we'll come back and see Peter, okay? Good luck with your show."

I glanced towards the cats in the cages and nodded my thanks, hoping they'd understand. Jasmine blinked at me, whiskers curled up. I looked around the crowded hall and tried to figure out our next steps.

"Do you think we can search the parking lot? Maybe someone stuffed her in a car."

"It's worth a shot," Ben said, standing again and shifting Gus. "Do you guys feel her?"

Gus leaned close to Ben's ear and whispered something that made Ben's eyes gleam. He turned to me, excited.

"He says he can feel she's close. Let's go."

We hurried out of the hall, avoiding the curious stare of the woman with the clipboard, and headed towards the parking lot. The day was getting warmer, and I worried about Razzy being locked in a car, sweltering in the heat. Panic made my feet move even faster.

"I'll start on this side if you want to go over there," I said, pointing to the other end. "Where did Sam go?"

"He's going through the tents to see if he can find her. Between all of us, we're bound to come across her."

I didn't voice my fear that he was wrong, but I could see my own worries reflected out of his eyes. He nodded, and we split up. I called to Razzy every few steps as I looked into each vehicle. Rudy's nose worked overtime as he tried to get a scent. He vaulted down and ran ahead, nose to the ground.

By the time Ben and I met up in the middle of the lot, I was drenched with sweat, and Rudy was flagging. I picked him back up and looked at Ben.

"We've got to keep looking. Both cats still feel her nearby."

"Let's go try to find Sam."

We walked back to the midway, and a surreal feeling pooling in my stomach that this was all just a horrible dream and soon I'd wake up. By the time we found Sam and saw by his face, he'd struck out too. That feeling faded, to be replaced with a sick sensation in my stomach.

"We'll go through them again," I said, not missing the look Sam and Ben exchanged. "She's got to be here. I won't stop until I find her."

"Hannah, you need to eat something."

"No! Not until I find my little girl."

I took off, tears streaming down my face, and began asking everyone I came across if they'd seen a Ragdoll cat. I didn't look back to see what Ben and Sam were doing. All that mattered was finding Razzy.

By the time I'd covered the entire vendor area twice, the sun sank in the west, and the lights for the fairgrounds flipped on. The boys were tired and no longer sure if they could feel their friend. Ben wrapped me in a hug and said the words I'd been dreading.

"We'd better go home. We'll start searching again in the morning."

I shook my head. It didn't matter how tired and hungry I was. What if Razzy was hungry and tired, too?

"No. I'm not going home. If we do that Ben... I have a terrible feeling I'll never see her again. Isn't there a nearby hotel?"

He nodded, his face drawn.

"Okay. That's a good idea. Let's get these guys some food and regroup. We're no good to Razzy if we're too tired to think straight."

I nodded and wiped my cheeks with the backs of my hands. Freya nodded as she began packing up her artwork.

"I'll look too, Hannah. We'll find her. We'll all help."

I looked towards Vera's tent and was surprised to see she'd already left. I hadn't even registered her packing up.

"Thanks, Freya. I'm sorry about earlier."

She flapped her hand and smiled.

"I overreacted. Chrissie's the only thing I've got. Her mom passed away last year and I'm trying to raise her, and not doing a great job."

Ben took my arm and steered me towards the alley that led to the parking lot. We'd spent hours searching for Razzy without coming across a single sign of her. I said a silent prayer as I looked up into the heavens. The stars winked into sight. She was out there, and somehow, some way, I was going to find her.

11

The morning sun filtered through the sheer curtain, lighting up the interior of the hotel room where we'd spent the night. From my spot in the uncomfortable chair, I could just make out Ben on the bed with Rudy and Gus snuggled up close. The poor boys had nearly collapsed when we'd checked in. They'd eaten their food before crawling onto the bed and crashing.

I turned my attention back to my phone, where I was going through the thousands of pictures I'd taken of Razzy over the years. I stopped on the newest one, where she was wearing the t-shirt I'd gotten her, and tears streamed down my face. I never thought I'd lose her. Not like this.

Ben moved in the bed, reaching for me, and his eyes flew open in a panic until they met mine.

"There you are. Are you okay?"

I backhanded the tears from my cheeks and nodded, not trusting my voice. He rolled over to face me.

"Did you get any sleep?"

"No," I said. My voice sounded like a rusty gate. "I tried, but I kept tossing and I didn't want to keep you guys awake."

"I'm sorry I fell asleep. I should've been awake for you."

He sat up and scrubbed at the back of his hair before yawning.

"It's okay. There's nothing we could do at night to find her. I've just been going through her pictures."

"Hannah, we're going to find her."

Rudy stretched from his spot on the bed next to Ben's legs and yawned widely. He thumped down and hopped on the chair, curling on top of my legs.

"Ma, I'm sorry we didn't see who took her. We were looking at something else. What I don't understand is why didn't she say something? We could've stopped it."

He began kneading my legs, his little face set in a morose expression. Gus peeked his head over Ben's shoulder.

"Good point, Rudy. We were so upset yesterday we didn't even think about it. Knowing her, she's using it to go undercover."

I sat straighter, an arm around Rudy to keep him from toppling over.

"You think it's related? That whoever murdered Tex kidnapped Razzy?"

Gus nodded, blinking his eyes. I glanced at Ben, a fresh fear gripping my heart. I hadn't even considered that. I'd thought only that someone saw how beautiful she was, assumed she was an expensive cat, and took her. The thought of my little girl being kept captive by a murderer was too much. I refused to even entertain the thought.

"Hannah..."

"I know. We've got to find her. Now that you're all awake, I'm going to call in. There's no way I'm going to work until she's found."

Ben nodded, but I didn't like the look haunting his eyes. The look that said, what if we never find her? Or worse. I turned away, blocking it out, and quickly dialed my boss, Tom Anderson.

"Hannah? What's up?"

"Hi, Tom. I just wanted to let you know I won't be in the office today. Something's come up."

"You still chasing that story down in Blanco Ridge? You've got a lot piling up on your assignment dock here. This better be good."

His gruff voice settled me. Tom was the best editor in Colorado, and more than that, he was a surrogate father-figure. Somehow, I told him everything that had happened and he listened. Once I was done, he cleared his throat.

"Take all the time you need. You'll find her, Hannah. I know how much she means to you. I also know that you'll move heaven and earth to get this done. You're unstoppable. You're chasing leads on this story and I won't put it down as vacation time, okay? Keep me updated."

"Thanks, Tom. You're the best. I don't know what I'd..."

"Stop right there. Don't let those thoughts in. They'll tear you apart. Find your cat and then get back to work."

I smiled as he barked out his commands, feeling immeasurably better. He ended the call, and I looked at Ben.

"He said..."

"I heard," Ben said, his mouth quirking into a smile. "With Tom, you never need to put him on speaker. Let's get some food into you and we'll get back to it."

"Yeah!" Rudy said, hopping down and stretching before clawing his nails in the rug. "Oops. Sorry."

I helped him untangle a claw from the rug's fibers and stood, feeling the crinks of a night curled in a hard chair.

"Let's do this."

We'd only booked the hotel room for one night, and slept in our clothes. Everything felt gritty as I quickly washed my face in the bathroom sink. I glanced in the mirror and looked away. If we didn't find Razzy today... we'd have to... I shook my head and dried my hands. If I thought like that, I'd have to acknowledge something I wasn't ready for. I didn't think I'd ever be ready for it.

Ben walked in and put his hands on my shoulders, resting his chin on the top of my head.

"Don't beat yourself up."

"How did you know I was?"

"I know you, sweetheart. We're going to do our best to find her. If I know her, she's doing her best to get back to us. We'll find her, Hannah. I feel it in my bones."

I nodded, unable to speak past the lump in my throat. I took a shuddering breath and leaned back against him.

"Let's grab something to eat on the way back to the fairgrounds. You ate hardly anything yesterday and you need your strength."

I nodded again, and we got the boys ready to go. I barely tasted the breakfast sandwich Ben pushed into my hand and tried chasing it with the bitter to-go coffee. Had Razzy eaten? Was she being cared for, or was she locked away, scared and alone? I bit my lip to keep my tears at bay.

Ben pulled into the parking lot of the fairgrounds and I noticed that, compared to the day before, it was nearly empty.

"How long does this festival run?"

"It's supposed to go all week and end next Sunday."

Our eyes met and understanding flashed between us. We needed to find Razzy before then. Way before then. I turned to look at the boys in the backseat. Rudy stared out the window.

"Do you sense her?"

He dipped his head and shook it slowly.

"Kind of? Like I can tell she's close, but I don't know exactly where. It's hard to describe. Maybe we can catch her scent. It will be a lot easier with fewer people around."

I unhooked my seat belt and paused.

"We should print up some flyers. I can probably make something with my phone. Does Canyon Falls have a print shop?"

Ben shook his head.

"I'm uncertain, but we can check. Let's look around and see if we can find any trace of her. If not, we'll go that route and start looking around the town. If someone local took her, she might be close."

"We can do what we did when we found you," Gus said, his deep voice soft. "Drive around until we strike gold."

I hoped it wouldn't come to that, but I would do whatever it took to bring my little girl home. I opened the door and let Rudy and Gus out of the backseat, keeping a firm hold on their leashes. Ben joined me and gently took Gus's lead.

"Should we split up to cover more ground?"

"Good idea. I'll head towards the midway if you want to check the fairground building. Maybe she got away, and she's hiding somewhere until she hears us."

Buoyed by the thought that she was close, Rudy and I headed towards the vendors. I still wasn't ready to believe she'd been taken by the murderer and all thoughts of trying to figure out who killed Tex were firmly in the background. We were early enough that the vendors were still getting set up. I spotted Freya and veered in her direction as Rudy trotted next to me, tail held high.

"No luck yet, huh?" Freya asked as soon as she saw me.

"No. Not yet. You've heard nothing from the other vendors?"

"Not a thing. We're all keeping an eye out. Chrissie's in school, but Burt's back. I saw him pull in a little while ago."

"Thanks, I'll go talk with him," I said, starting off, only to come to a quick stop when I saw someone else at Vera's tent. "Who's that?"

Freya turned around, shading her eyes from the sun.

"Oh, that's Patty. I think that's her sister. I didn't even notice earlier. Vera must not be coming in today. That's weird. I've never known her to miss a day in all the years I've been doing this. You know how she is. Some days it would be nice to get a break from her, especially during a long run like this festival."

Suspicion prickled down my spine as I nodded at Freya and crossed the short distance to Vera's tent. Patty resembled her sister, especially around the eyes, but she at least smiled as I approached. She was much taller than her sister and towered over me.

"What a beautiful cat. It's too bad my sister isn't here. She loves cats."

"She saw them yesterday. In fact, we're back here because we're missing one of our cats. She was taken yesterday," I said, fumbling in my pocket for my phone. "Here's a picture of her. Have you seen her?"

Patty smiled as she took the phone with one hand and used the other to bring the glasses hanging around her neck up to peer through them.

"Oh my, she's gorgeous. I haven't seen her, but I'll keep an eye out. Did she run off or something?"

"No, she was taken. Her leash was cut. Where's Vera?"

Patty handed my phone back and gave me a sunny smile.

"She had some things she had to do to today, and she asked me to fill in for her. I think she's planning on coming back this afternoon. Did you need something?"

"No, I just had a few questions for her. Does she live locally?"

"She's got a place in Blanco Ridge. Why?"

Her sunny smile dimmed in wattage, and she took a step back. I must have come on too strong.

"Oh, just curious. I bought a few things from her the other day and I was wondering if she took custom orders."

Patty's face cleared, but she shook her head.

"No, these are all ordered in. Try back after lunch. If you'll excuse me, I need to get back to setting things up."

She turned away, and I stared at her back. Why had Vera picked today to miss the festival? I walked towards Burt's food truck when I heard a familiar voice calling my name. I turned and nearly fell over as I saw my best friend, Ashley Wilson, jogging towards me, hauling a huge bag.

"Girl, there you are," she said, coming to a stop and putting her hand on her chest. "Whew, I need to get to the gym more often. Baby weight is one thing, but I'm out of shape. Come here, sweetie. Tom told me what happened, and I came down as fast as my car could drive."

She pulled me into a hug and the tears I'd been holding back flooded out. Rudy pawed at my leg.

"Ma?"

I gave Ashley another squeeze, wiped my eyes, and scooped him up.

"Thank you so much for coming. You didn't have to do that."

"Are you kidding? Razzy is my niece. I can't believe you didn't call me."

"I'm sorry, Ash. I've been so..."

"I get it, sweetie. I'm here and we're gonna find her," she said, before pulling a stack of papers out of her bag. "I used the newsroom printer to run off a bunch of flyers. Even Vinnie helped. Everyone's pulling for you. I used the spare key you got me and brought you and a change of clothes."

The news that Vinnie Mangione, my arch-nemesis at work, had pitched in, coupled with her thoughtfulness, threatened to bring the tears back, but I blinked them away.

"You're the best, Ash."

Another familiar voice hollered my name, and I looked over my shoulder to see Anastasia Aspen and her fiancé, Robert, coming our way.

"And I called in some backup," Ashley said with a wink. "I figured she'd be able to help in ways that I can't. I don't know everything she can do, but I know Anastasia is a wonder."

Anastasia was dressed, as always, in a flowing shirt and ornate top, and her red hair looked like a cloud of flame as the sun hit it. Robert stood back as Anastasia pulled me into a hug.

"Have faith, dear. Things are not as dark as they seem. We'll find her."

Anastasia shared my ability to communicate with cats, and it was thanks to her and the gift of a special necklace that also enabled Ben to talk with them. She had helped me in innumerable ways in the past, and here she was again.

"Where's Callie?" Rudy asked, squiggling as his head popped up between us.

Anastasia laughed and smoothed his fur with her hand. Rudy had a bit of a crush on the beautiful calico cat Anastasia had adopted from the Valewood Resort clowder. She'd been just a kitten when she'd gone to live with Anastasia, but she was growing like a weed.

"I didn't even see you, sweet boy. She's at home and not too happy about it. But you know what a whirlwind she is."

Anastasia winked at me and waved Robert forward.

"We're here to assist in any way we can. The more people we have looking for Razzy, the quicker we'll find her. Where's Ben?"

I looked behind her and spotted Ben coming our way, and noticed that we were the center of attention of all the vendors.

"He's coming. I can't thank you enough for coming down here. I can't believe it."

"So, where do we start? I read your piece about the murder. Do you think it's related?" Ashley asked.

"It could be. I don't want to think that, though."

Anastasia's face darkened, and she nodded, before leaning close.

"The spirits warned me that this web is twisted. We will need to use care as we untangle all the threads. Someone is not as they seem."

She had that right. I had a bad feeling that many of the vendors were not as they seemed. Ben walked up, and I waited while everyone exchanged greetings. My mind kept going back to Vera. Something told me I needed to find her.

"Ben, can you pull up your app on your phone? The background one from your investigator toolkit? I need to find where Vera lives."

Four sets of curious human eyes and two sets of cat eyes swiveled in my direction as I quickly outlined my suspicions, dropping my voice so Patty wouldn't overhear. Ben nodded and produced an address tied to Vera's name. I took a picture with my phone as an idea came to me.

"Ashley, do you want to go with me and see if we can track Vera down?"

"Shouldn't I go with you?" Ben asked.

I shook my head and looked around.

"No. Just in case she's still here, it makes sense to split up. I'll take Rudy, and you keep Gus. One of them is bound to sense Razzy, and each team should have one cat."

My friends all nodded and shared hopeful smiles. Ashley passed around the fliers she'd printed and kept back half the stack.

"You can pass these out and we'll put them up in Blanco Ridge," she said.

Ben gave her a quick hug.

"We've got a plan. I see Burt waving at us. I'd better go talk to him. I know he wasn't here yesterday, but maybe he's heard something."

He gave me a quick kiss on the cheek before walking off, Robert next to him. Anastasia held back, her eyes never leaving my face.

"Be careful where you go. I sense danger lurking where you do not expect it."

And with that cheery note, Ashley took my arm and led me back towards the parking lot. I was used to Anastasia's dire warnings, but this one hit differently. This time, my Razzy girl was in danger, and I didn't like it one bit. Ashley chattered as we walked, but my mind was full of dark threads that muted her words. I hoped I wasn't chasing after the wrong thing, but something, deep down, told me I was on the right track.

12

*A*shley kept me entertained with stories of my honorary niece while I drove towards Blanco Ridge. Even though I had a strict rule about cats staying either in the backseat or the passenger side while I drove, today, I made an exception. Rudy cuddled on my lap, his whiskers brushing my arms every so often. His warm fur calmed my nerves a little, and took my mind off the fear that threatened to gnaw away at my stomach.

"So, tell me about Vera."

"Um, I know little about her. She's not the nicest person I've ever met. She was married to Tex, the man who was killed, but they weren't married long. We're trying to see if she had any motive to want him dead."

"You mean, besides being his ex-wife?" Ashley said with a chuckle. "For some people, that's all the motive they'd ever need."

I turned to glance at her before focusing back on the road. I conjured up an image of the sour woman and agreed with Ashley.

"I wonder how she felt about Tex's relationship with Sheila?"

"Who's that?"

I brought Ashley up to speed on the inner-workings of the vendor's lives and she nodded, eyes wide.

"Who would have thought it'd be better than a soap opera? So, we have an ex-wife and an ex-girlfriend working within yards of each other. Honestly, I'm surprised it wasn't one of them who was killed. What was Tex like?"

"I never met him, but from what we've learned, he was well-liked, jovial. Loved to cook and apparently was very good at it. I haven't been able to find any sign that he was the one stealing Burt's recipes or tools, though. It's the oddest thing."

"He was likely being set up. And who better to make him pay than an ex-lover? Have you found out why his relationship with Sheila didn't work out?"

Ashley preferred the fluffy lifestyle stories that she was assigned on our paper, but that didn't mean she have a nose for crime. In fact, I think her constant immersion into the weddings and gossip of Golden Hills made her better at sniffing out crimes of passion than anyone else.

"No, and you're absolutely right. I'm slipping. I was focusing on the wrong thing, and now my cat's gone and I can't focus on anything at all."

"And that is likely intentional. You brought them with you yesterday, right?"

"Yes. We went everywhere on the grounds. Everyone would've seen her."

"Do you think anyone overheard you talking with her? I don't mean that they'd understand, but I can hear them meowing back to you when you talk to them. Is it possible someone put two and two together?"

I grimaced as I turned off the highway onto the side street that would take us to Vera's address.

"Yes. That's partly why I'm focusing so hard on Vera. We were standing next to her tent yesterday while I talked with the cats. We thought it was safe, but she kept looking at us oddly. Oh gosh, Ash, do you think I endangered Razzy? What if someone wants to run tests on her or something? I never even thought of that."

Ashley's face folded into a frown, and she touched my arm.

"I'm sorry. I didn't want you to take it like that. I'm just tossing out theories. Honestly, if I had to guess, the killer knew you were onto them and they nabbed Razzy to throw you off and keep your focus from the investigation. They want you distracted so you don't find out the truth. I bet you they're planning to make a break for it."

I didn't answer her as I stared at the empty lot where Vera's house should have been, a sick feeling pooling in my stomach. I checked the map and confirmed the coordinates were correct.

"Well, if this isn't suspicious, I don't know what is. Why is this an empty lot?"

Ashley unbuckled her seat belt and opened the door and before I could blink, Rudy was out in a flash, darting over her lap. She let out a startled eep and lunged for him, too late.

"Oh gosh, he won't run off, will he? Dear Lord, I can't be responsible for you losing another cat."

Rudy had stopped in the middle of the lot, nose to the ground like a bloodhound.

"No, he won't run off, but I'd better get over there," I said, leaving the engine to run as I got out. "Rudy, what are you doing?"

He didn't answer as he trotted back and forth, sniffing everything. Ashley joined me, bumping me with her arm as she looked around before pointing.

"There. Let's go ask that neighbor."

I walked over and scooped up a protesting Rudy and followed Ashley across the weather-beaten, weedy lot.

"Ma, I was onto something."

"We'll go back. Let's do a little asking around first."

Ashley walked up the rickety steps and eased away from the railing that looked like a loud sneeze would crumple the rusty iron. She searched for a doorbell before knocking sharply. We waited, listening for movement within.

"There's a car parked in front, so I'm sure someone's home," Ashley said, before she knocked again.

"Hold your horses."

The voice inside sounded like it belonged to a very irritated person and my suspicion was confirmed as it opened a crack, still secured by a chain. What little I could see revealed an older woman, with tightly curled iron-gray hair.

"Whaddya want? I ain't got money to buy nothing, and I've already found God."

Ashley smiled and deployed the full force of her personality. The other woman blinked.

"We just need a moment of your time. Do you know anything about the woman who owns the lot next door?"

"Might. What's it worth to you? My time doesn't come cheap."

It was my turn to blink. Did I have any cash on me? Ashley swooped in and saved the day.

"I've got fifty bucks in my wallet that could go into your wallet. Mind you," she said, holding up a hand. "The information better be true. What's your name? I'm Ashley and this is Hannah."

There was silence behind the door for a moment before the chain was removed and the door swung open to reveal a woman, shorter than me, wearing a faded housecoat, the type I hadn't seen since I was a little girl.

"Elaine. Alright. But you can't come in. I don't let strange people in my house. Is that a bobcat you're holding?"

Her hand went up to grip the neckline of her housecoat and I shook my head, turning Rudy so she could see his face.

"No, he's a Ragdoll. He's a big cat, but he is very sweet."

Rudy blinked his blue eyes at the woman. She visibly thawed and reached a trembling hand towards him. Her wrinkled skin looked as thin as rice paper. He gently bumped her hand with the top of his fuzzy head, and she relaxed a little.

"Oh, he's so soft. Like a rabbit."

If Razzy had been on the receiving end of that backhanded compliment, she would have bristled in indignation. I had to swallow hard to keep a sob from erupting from my chest. Ashley seemed to sense my struggle and patted my arm.

"Do you know if a woman named Vera lived next door?" she asked, pointing towards the vacant lot.

"Yeah, she used to. Had an old single wide that made the neighborhood look like trash. The city tore it down, finally. It must have been about two years ago. It sat vacant for so long, I thought it was going to fall down. Racoons were living in it. It stunk to high heaven."

"Elaine, have you seen her since then?" I asked.

"Nah, she moved out when she married that fat man. I can't remember his name. Anyway, that was the last I saw of her, and good riddance. She was always screaming at the top of her lungs at him when they were dating. What on earth possessed a man like that to marry her? Nasty woman," she said with a shudder. "He seemed nice, though. He used to bring me a few meals. Said he had leftovers from his food truck and didn't want them to go to waste. She'd carp at him about wasting food on the likes of me. No, she's long gone and I don't miss her. Honestly, the racoons were better neighbors than she was."

My heart sank as I realized we'd truly reached a dead end. Vera hadn't been in here in years and we had no other address for her.

Ashley dug in her wallet and handed over two crisp twenties and a ten. Elaine reached for it, her hand trembling, but she paused.

"I haven't asked why you're looking for Vera? You're not hit women, are you? I saw that in one of my shows."

"No, we're not hit women. My other cat, Razzy, went missing, and we had reason to believe Vera was behind it. She looks a lot like this one, if you see her. She went missing at the fairgrounds in Canyon Falls."

I pulled a flyer out of my bag and passed it over to Elaine. Her hand trembled slightly as she held it up to peer at it.

"Oh, what a shame. I'm so sorry. I hope you find her. I don't want your money," Elaine said, but her eyes looked longingly at the cash in Ashley's hand. "It wouldn't be right."

"Nonsense," Ashley said, pushing the money into Elaine's hand. "We had an agreement. Thank you for your time. If you think of anything else, Hannah will give you her card."

I juggled Rudy around as I dug into my bag and found one of my cards for her. Elaine peered at the writing and looked at me closely.

"Newspaper reporter, huh? Will wonders never cease? In my day, we were all homemakers. Good for you. I hope you find your cat."

She gripped the cash in her hand and gave us a jerky head nod before popping back into her house, closing the door and replacing the chain. I sighed and trudged back down the steps, staring at the vacant lot as if Vera's trailer would magically appear.

"Well, what do we do now?" Ashley asked as we got into my Blazer.

"I don't know. We could go to the county and talk to the auditor, but if she rents, that won't do us any good. I wonder if Ray would know. It's a small enough town. He probably knows everyone and their relations going back a generation or two."

"Well, let's go talk to him. We won't rest until Razzy is safe and sound, back in your arms. We can also put up a few of these flyers. Just in case."

Rudy vaulted into the backseat and stared at Elaine's house as we drove away.

"She was lonely," he said, his voice soft.

I looked at him in the rearview mirror and nodded.

"You're right, bud. I hope she's getting enough to eat. She seemed so thin and frail. I wonder if she has any relatives?"

"Well, while we're talking to Ray, let's see if there's a town project for senior meals," Ashley said as she listened to my end of the conversation. "I bet she's too proud to take charity, but those programs do a great job."

I nodded as my dash lit up with an incoming call from Ben. I hit the button and his voice came over the speakers.

"Hannah, are you in Blanco Ridge yet? Did you find Vera?"

"No, it was a dead-end. Her lot's here, but there's nothing on it. Her sister flat out lied to me. What's up?"

"I just talked to Burt, and he knew Tex's attorney. He's got an office there in town. I'll text you the address. It's worth a shot to see if you can find out more about Tex's will while you're there. I asked Ray, and he doesn't have a problem with it. He said he can't give us the info, but if the lawyer wants to, that's fine."

"Sure, we'll do that. Is Ray in town, or is he out there?"

"He's here, why?"

"See if he knows anything about where Vera lives. Oh, and can you ask him if there's a senior meal program for residents of Blanco Ridge?"

If Ben was thrown by my conversational switch, he didn't let on. I could feel his smile through the phone.

"Of course. Tell me later. Anastasia might be onto something with Razzy. I've got to go."

He ended the call as I squawked in frustration. What did Anastasia mean? Ashley took my hand.

"It's okay, Hannah. If anyone can find her, Anastasia will. Let's go talk to that lawyer. Between the two of us, I bet we can charm the intel right out of him."

My phone dinged with Ben's text and I passed it over to Ashley to find the address, while my mind spun. I knew Anastasia had special gifts and my friend was right. Just because we hadn't found Razzy here didn't mean the trip was wasted. I no longer hid from the thought that whoever kidnapped Razzy was a murderer. It was the only thing that made sense.

13

The town of Blanco Ridge had changed little since my last visit several months ago. Its stark contrast to Golden Hills was never more apparent as I drove down the main street and noticed all the boarded-up shops and for lease signs. Ashley sighed as we pulled into a parking space.

"Wow. I didn't realize this town had been hit so hard. There's not much left, is there?"

"Not really. It's happening in a lot of small towns and I don't think anyone knows how to fix it. The kids all leave after graduation and there just aren't enough people to start small businesses and keep them running."

"Are you sure this is the right place?" Rudy asked from the backseat. "It looks abandoned."

He wasn't wrong. The sign proclaimed we were at the offices of Bradburn Legal, but the place looked unkempt and a little seedy. I exchanged a glance with Ashley and nodded.

"I think so, bud. Only one way to find out. Let's head inside. I'm going to put you in your carrier, just in case. Remember to be quiet. Not everyone appreciates it when I bring my cat along."

"I know the drill, Ma," he said, grumbling under his breath as he slid into his bag.

I didn't need to translate for Ashley. She got the gist just fine and laughed merrily as she opened her door.

The door opened and once inside, I wasn't sure what I'd expected, but I didn't expect to be looking at an office that could have come right off the set of a 1940s film noir movie. A desk that had to be older than me, and possibly my father, sat off to the side, surrounding by shelves groaning under the weight of books that had to be just as ancient.

There was no one else in the cramped space until a door popped open and an older man came out, looking just as startled as we were. He slicked his hand over his thinning, dark hair and gave me a puzzled look.

"Do you have an appointment?"

"No, but if you're not too busy, we just have a few questions for you."

He heaved a tired sigh and sank into the cracked leather chair behind the desk, motioning towards the rickety chairs across from him. I would have preferred to remain standing, but I sank down anyway, praying the chair would hold my weight. I tucked Rudy under my seat while Ashley set her phasers to charm.

She held a hand across the desk and unleashed a smile that had melted more than one man's heart in her day.

"Hello. I'm Ashley Wilson, and this is my friend, Hannah Murphy. I'm so grateful you don't mind taking a few minutes out of your busy day for us."

He blinked, his brown eyes locked with hers, and a flush crept up his neck. Ashley was a statuesque goddess when she didn't even try, but when she did, I didn't think there was a man alive who could resist her. Thank goodness she'd come with us.

"I'm Ralph Bradburn. What can I do for you lovely ladies?" he asked as his glance slid off of me before fastening back on Ashley. "Are you looking for a divorce lawyer?"

Ashley giggled and dimpled before shaking her head.

"No. I'm afraid not."

Was he disappointed? He sure looked like he was as his eyes darted to the rings on Ashley's left hand.

"Then what can I do for you? You're not local. I know most of the people in this town. Trust me, I'd remember someone like you."

I broke in, much to Ralph's annoyance.

"We're working for Burt Younkin. You've heard about what happened?"

His face fell as he nodded his head and leaned back in his chair, placing his hands protectively over his paunch. I wondered if he knew his tie was stained.

"Yes, but I'm uncertain how I can be of any help to you. I've already answered the police's questions. The deceased and Mr. Younkin are clients of mine, and I can't share any information about my clients with anyone."

Ashley leaned forward and if Ralph had been a cartoon character, his eyes would've bugged out of his head and dove into her v-necked shirt.

"But we're only trying to help Mr. Younkin," she said, softening her voice. "You see, even though the police released him, there's still a lot of suspicion surrounding him. We were hoping you wouldn't mind going over the contents of Tex's will with us. It will be public record soon, so it's not like you're doing anything wrong."

"I'm afraid I don't follow your logic."

"If we can prove Burt doesn't have a motive in wanting Tex dead, that would go a long way towards helping him. And not just with the police. I'm sure he's having a difficult time with the other vendors, particularly because of the way Tex was killed," I said, noticing his eyes never left Ashley's expansive cleavage.

"Well, I don't know... I already sent a copy of the will over to the police."

"Perfect," Ashley said, clapping her hands together lightly. "Then it's no big deal to share them with us as well. We'd appreciate it very much, Mr. Bradburn."

He practically salivated all over his desk.

"Please. Call me Ralph. I suppose you're right. I could let you have a little peek, but you'll have to promise not to reveal the contents to anyone else."

"It will be our little secret, Ralph."

I rolled my eyes as Ralph sprang up and walked over to the lengthy row of cabinets along the wall. He returned, carrying a file bursting at the seams. I couldn't resist scooting forward in my seat as he opened the file. I'd developed the skill of reading upside down as a curious child, and it had served me well in my job as a reporter.

He fiddled with the papers, seemingly reluctant to hand them over, even though he'd gotten this far. His internal struggle was stamped on his face as he darted a glance outside and finally passed the will over to Ashley. I noticed that the sheet below it carried the logo of a popular life insurance firm in our area, and my fingers itched to snatch the paper away from the folder.

"Oh, it's very simple. Pete gets the house and the food truck business," she said. "Who is Sheila Bream?"

"Sheila?" I asked, blinking in surprise. "She runs the food truck that sat next to Tex. They were briefly involved."

If Ralph seemed surprised by my knowledge, he said nothing, but nodded instead.

"They'd planned to wed. Tex filed this new will a few months ago."

"Did he remove Vera Paddington and replace her with Sheila?"

That surprised him. Ralph blinked a few times.

"How did you know?"

"Educated guess. Is there any way Vera would've known she was removed from the will? Is she one of your clients, too?"

A look of distaste flitted across Ralph's features, but he quickly masked it with an oily smile.

"No, I did not have the pleasure of representing Miss Bradenton. And to answer your question, it's not my job to inform someone if they are no longer a beneficiary. I leave that to my clients, if they want to. Are you insinuating...?"

"We're just putting out feelers," I said, quickly cutting him off. "Do you know Vera well?"

The look of distaste was back and this time, he didn't bother to hide it.

"I do not."

His words tumbled like a lead balloon, and he refused to say anything more. He stretched out his hand towards Ashley.

"May I have that back, please?"

"Of course," she said, dimpling again. "Thank you so much. You've been such a tremendous help to us."

He visibly expanded with pride at her praise and slicked his hand over his head again.

"Anything for a lovely lady like yourself."

Hmph, I thought, nearly snorting over his refusal to use the plural. Ashley stood, uncrossing her legs slowly, and turned to leave. She stopped and unleashed that smile one more time.

"Just one more thing, Ralph?"

"Yes?"

"Would you know who the beneficiary of Tex's life insurance is?"

He glanced down at the papers in the file folder and winced.

"I shouldn't..."

"Oh, I won't tell anyone," she said. "We'll have two little secrets, Ralph."

"Vera Paddington is the named beneficiary. I can't reveal how much the policy is, though."

"Thank you, Ralph. It was such a pleasure meeting you. You've done us a huge favor."

He pushed back from his desk too quickly. His chair nearly toppled over as he fumbled on the corner of his desk where his cards lay.

"Here," he said, rushing around the corner of the desk. "If you ever need anything, call me. Day or night."

She tucked the card away in her palm and nodded.

"I will. Thank you again, Ralph."

She breezed out, and I followed in her wake, completely unnoticed by Ralph, as he moved to stare at Ashley through the grimy window that faced the street. I glanced at Rudy through the mesh window of his bag and snorted again. I could've paraded a zoo of animals through Ralph's office and he would've never noticed.

I slid into the driver's seat after stowing Rudy in the back and cranked the key to fire up the engine. Ashley put on her seatbelt and waggled her fingers in a wave towards Ralph's office as I pulled away from the curb.

"Still got it," she said, looking at the card with distaste. "I'm not sure I want it, but I definitely still have it."

"All I've got to say is thank goodness you were with me," I said as I turned down a side street. "If it had just been me, I would've been dead in the water."

"You know how I feel about water baths," Rudy said from the backseat. "But that guy made me want one. With extra shampoo."

I translated for Ashley, and she threw her head back in a laugh before looking back at him.

"Same little one, same. Well, at least we know what we're dealing with. Tell me more about Sheila. If she knew about the will, she's got the best motive of all. Tex was worth a mint."

I glanced over in shock as I pulled over, next to an enormous tree that shaded the street.

"Really?"

"Yeah. Sheila's going to be a millionaire a few times over."

My mouth fell open.

"Sorry. Did you say multi-millionaire?"

"Yes, ma'am. I'm in the wrong line of work. If I knew running a barbecue truck came with that kind of money, I wouldn't have even bothered getting a degree in journalism."

"But then we'd never have met and you wouldn't be having adventures like this."

"True. Very true. Ah well. I'm happy with my lot in my life. Everything's turned out the way it was meant to."

"Poor Tex can't say the same thing," I said. "I never really suspected Sheila, but now..."

"If he was worth that much, I wonder how much his life insurance policy is?" Rudy asked.

"Maybe we can find that out from Ray. It looks like way too many people had financial motive to want Tex out of the picture. I wonder if Vera knew she was out of the will. I still think there's something up with her."

"Well, maybe she'll be back at the fairgrounds. You said her sister mentioned she was tied up with something. With any luck, she'll be there, and we'll find out if she had anything to do with Razzy's disappearance."

My heart ached at the mention of her name. We weren't getting any closer to finding out who'd taken her, even though we were making progress figuring out who'd killed Tex. Suddenly, I hoped Ashley was right, and the murderer was the one who'd grabbed Razzy. If not, I did not know how I was going to find her. But I wouldn't rest until I did. No matter what. I pulled back onto the street and we put up some flyers before heading back to the fairgrounds.

14

ust puffed up underneath my feet as Ashley and I walked from the parking lot back to the midway. I felt as though I could make the trek with my eyes closed. Weariness made my feet feel like they weighed five hundred pounds a piece, but I knew until I got Razzy home, sleep would not come. Rudy shifted in his bag as though he could feel what I was going through.

"Burt Younkin. What's he like?" Ashley asked. "I mean, the murder weapon is his and his prints were on it, so honestly, he should still be a suspect."

"I know. I'm sure for Sam and Ray, he's the number one suspect. But I just don't think he did it. He was with us while Tex was being killed. And honestly? He's a really nice guy."

"Well, that's good."

I glanced over at Ashley and saw she was wearing her trademark grin.

"Why?"

"Because I'm starving and green chiles sound very good. If he was the murderer, it would make it very awkward to purchase food from him. Particularly if he thought we were on to him. And before you say you're not hungry, I know you are. You've got to eat, Hannah."

When would everyone stop forcing food in my direction? I knew she meant well, but the lead weight sitting in the bottom of my stomach wasn't going anywhere. And likely, it wouldn't until I heard her familiar voice say, "Mama."

I didn't say any of that, though. I merely nodded and murmured something about trying. I barely paid attention. All of my attention was fixed on Vera Bradenton, who I spotted standing next to her sister, beneath her tent. I picked up the pace.

Ashley paused before hurrying to catch up with me.

"That's her?" she asked, huffing a little as she kept up. "I pictured someone different."

"That's Vera. Rudy, get your sniffer ready. I can't shake the feeling that she's the one who took Razzy."

I quickly closed the distance and something in my expression must have been awful enough that Vera stepped back, putting her much taller sister between us.

"I've been looking for you," I said, fighting to keep my tone normal.

"Really? Why? Are you not happy with your purchase? All sales are final. It says so right there, by the register."

She jabbed her finger over her shoulder while a smirk curled her lips. I wasn't a violent person, but right then, I longed to wipe the smile off her face. Ashley's fingers curled around my arm, signaling to dial it back a notch, but I wasn't interested.

"Actually, I'm trying to find my cat. She disappeared yesterday. Right before you left."

"Well, that's too bad," she said, while her sister looked on with a raised eyebrow. "You should probably keep a better eye on your animals. Parading them around like you do, it's no wonder one of them got away. You're lucky you haven't lost all three."

I erased the distance between us and stared her down. It didn't matter that she was a few inches taller than I and had probably seventy-five pounds on me.

"What do you mean by that? Was that a threat?"

Patty shoved her arm between us, a frown crinkling her face.

"Vera, this isn't like you. I know how much you love cats and how devastated you'd be if one of them disappeared. Show a little compassion."

Vera's face was devoid of anything resembling compassion, empathy, or any human emotion. Her eyes were flat as she sneered at me.

"Exactly. And I take good care of my cats. I don't expose them to danger. Or stick my nose in where it doesn't belong."

"I'm sorry, ladies, but my sister isn't feeling well. I need to get her out of the sun," Patty said, giving Vera a little shove. "I hope you find your cat, miss."

She ushered her sister back into the tent, leaving me seething at the edge of the midway. I wanted nothing more than to follow and scream at the woman until she cracked and admitted she'd done it. Ashley's grip tightened, and she tugged me away.

"Not now. I think you're right, though. That miserable woman knows something. I can tell," she said.

"She said something right after Tex was killed, too," I said, lowering my voice. "She said something about him deserving it. I think she killed him and I think she took Razzy. Rudy, did you smell anything?"

He shook his eye, blue eyes brimming with sadness.

"All I could smell was disinfectant. It made my nose hurt."

"See, she has Razzy, and she made sure we couldn't track her," I said, straining at Ashley's grip.

"Honey, you can't prove it, and you won't get Razzy back by antagonizing that awful woman."

Something in Ashley's tone made me blink and come back to myself. I knew she was right, but I couldn't think straight. It was all just too much. A sob tore at my throat and she folded me into a hug.

"Girl, it's gonna be okay. You've got to be strong."

I nodded and wiped my tears away with the back of my hand while Rudy shifted at my feet. I scooped him up, burying my face in his fur, just like I always did with Razzy. It wasn't the same, but it helped. He purred deep within his chest, trying to soothe me.

"I'm sorry. I don't know what came over me. We've got to work to prove she did it. I don't know how, but we've got to try."

"There's my Hannah. Okay, here's what we're gonna do. We're gonna go get something to eat, and then we're gonna talk to Sheila and feel her out," Ashley said, striding ahead. "No wonder you love the crime beat. This is invigorating!"

I heard Ben's voice calling my name and hurried in his direction. Burt stood next to him, flanked by Anastasia and Robert. Gus let out a low-pitched yowl as we got closer and Rudy pulled at his lead until they met, sniffing each other. Ben opened his arms, and I practically dove into them, resting my head against his broad chest.

"We didn't find her, but we learned a few things," Ashley said, greeting everyone. "You must be Burt Younkin. I've heard you're one heck of a cook."

I stepped back and noticed Burt's face was red as he looked up into Ashley's eyes.

"I'd like to think so. Whatever you'd like, Miss, is yours, at no cost. I'd like to feed your whole crew. Hannah, I'm so sorry to hear about your cat. All of us vendors will do everything we can to help."

"Chrissie and I put up a bunch of flyers, and Freya went to town and copied some more. We're going to plaster them everywhere."

My throat clenched with emotion as I nodded at Gerald. Ashley put a hand on her hip and tilted her head.

"All but one of you, anyway. We just talked to Vera, and she's anything but helpful."

"Oh, that's just Vera," Burt said, waving a hand. "She's always been a hedgehog. I've never known someone as nasty as her. Don't take offense, that's just her way."

He moved to join Gerald at the counter, firing off orders that had the young man scrambling to do his bidding. Was Burt right? Was Vera just a desperately unhappy person who took out her anger at everyone she met? Or was she a cat stealing murderer? I looked towards her tent and shuddered as I realized she was staring at us. Had she overheard us?

Anastasia skirted the knot of people standing in front of Burt's truck and took my arm.

"Hannah, it's going to be okay. I know it doesn't feel like it right now, but you're getting closer. I can sense it. She's close and she's okay."

Relief flooded through me from my head to my toes as I gasped sharply.

"You can feel her? Where is she?"

"Not directly," Anastasia said, holding up a finger that nearly crushed my hopes. "But she is well. And if I know her, she's working hard to figure out how to get free and find you. Have faith, Hannah. All will be well."

I barely knew what to do with her words. Typically, Anastasia tended more towards the doom and gloom side of things. This positivity kept my fragile hopes alive.

Ben passed me a burger loaded with green chiles and gave me a stern look.

"Eat every bite. You need your strength."

I won't say my appetite had returned, but the burger disappeared faster than I thought it could, and everyone was right. It helped me feel better. I listened as Ashley filled everyone in on our trip to Blanco Ridge. Burt guffawed at her description of Ralph Bradburn.

"That's Ralphie in a nutshell. The poor sap's never been married, which is probably a good thing. I don't think he could ever be faithful to one woman. He's a decent lawyer, though."

I'd have to take his word for it, because I didn't believe it for a second, but I kept that to myself. I turned as everyone kept talking and watched Sheila across the way. Her truck was busy as people crowded around, carrying away their loaded baked potatoes. She was alone, and she kept darting looks towards our little gathering. I pulled Ben aside, making sure the cats stayed close.

"Sheila inherits all of Tex's money. Besides, what's earmarked for the food truck, that is."

"Really?" Ben said, his eyes tracking towards her. "That's..."

"Odd? I agree. According to Ralph, they were planning on getting married. Which puts her entire act of not mentioning their involvement in a whole new light. We need to talk to her."

"Let's wait until she's not so busy. It's too easy for her to brush us off. In the meantime, I'll go back to the car and use my laptop to search for her background. I'll use the fairground's Wi-Fi."

I glanced down at the cats, who were flagging, even though they desperately wanted to hide it.

"That's a good idea. I'd take both boys and let them get a nap while you work. It's clear Razzy isn't here, and they need their rest."

Burt had made the boys a special burger with no seasoning, and they'd split it. Now that their tummies were full, Gus and Rudy's eyes were heavy. And they weren't the only ones. I could tell Ashley missed Gracie, and she kept looking at her phone. As much as I appreciated my friend's support, it was time for her to head back home. I patted Ben's arm and headed her way.

"Ash, I..."

"Nope. Don't even say it. Gracie's with Dan, having the time of her life being spoiled by him. I'll go home in a few hours, but not yet. We've still got a cat to find."

Her willingness to help brought tears to my eyes, and I blinked quickly to clear them. I'd turned into a watering pot.

"Thank you, Ash. We want to talk to Sheila over there, but now's not the time. Ben's going back to the car with the boys to do a little searching for her. I'm not sure what to do in the meantime."

"That horrible woman has to live somewhere," she said, looking back at Vera's tent. "I'm guessing someone knows where. If not, we'll follow her when she leaves for the day. With any luck, she'll lead us right to Razzy. Let's ask around. I'll start with Burt."

She turned and smiled at the food truck owner, who looked dazzled. He blinked several times.

"Yes?"

"I was just wondering if you knew where Vera lived, sweetie. We're having a terrible time trying to find her house."

He shook his head and sighed.

"I don't, I'm sorry. I heard you were looking for her in Blanco

Ridge. As far as I know, that's where she lives. She's got a travel trailer, though. She got that from her divorce with Tex. To be honest, once they split-up, I paid her little attention. There's a bunch of RV parks around. You could try looking through those."

This was news to me and made me wish we'd asked Ralph for the divorce papers he had for Tex. What else did she get from him? I was lost in thought as Sam Trotter approached and jumped when he tapped my arm.

"Any luck?"

"No, Sam. Nothing yet. How about you?"

"We're still looking. Ray said that address Ben found didn't pan out, huh?"

"Yep. It's a vacant lot."

"That's odd. He checked and said that was the address she gave him when we questioned her. He's looking into it. Since she's back, we're going to be interviewing her again. It's suspicious she gave us the wrong address."

I opened my mouth to request to be in on the interview, but Sam shook his head with a sad grin.

"I'm sorry, Hannah. Cops only. We've got to do this by the book."

I nodded, understanding, even though I really didn't want to. Ashley turned and smiled at Sam.

"Wow, I didn't know police officers were available in this model. Ashley Wilson."

Sam flushed as he shook her hand.

"Sam Trotter. My wife, Coleen, always reads your column in the Post. She loves how you describe weddings and such. She'll be so jealous I got to meet you."

"I'd love to meet Coleen. She sounds wonderful."

I tuned out their conversation and looked over at Sheila again. The lunch rush had petered out, and she was by herself. I said goodbye to Ben and the boys as they headed to the parking lot and walked over to Sheila by myself. Something told me she was involved in Tex's death somehow, and I was determined to find out how.

15

*T*he smile on Sheila's face dropped when she saw me approach, but I didn't let that slow me down. Something was odd here, and I was going to find out what it was. No matter what. I gave her a sunny smile and leaned against the counter.

"Looks like you're having a good day today. Plenty of customers."

The look on her face clearly said she'd rather be talking to anyone else but me, but she grudgingly nodded her head before looking down at the counter and wiping at an invisible spot. Since that was one of my coping mechanisms, I knew she just needed to keep her hands busy, and forged ahead. This time I needed to ask an open-ended question, one that demanded a response. One that she didn't expect.

"When did you start your food truck?"

Sheila blinked a few times before twisting the rag between her hands.

"About five years ago, I guess. Why?"

"I was wondering how long you knew Tex before you got involved with him. It's too bad that the relationship didn't work out. I'm not engaged, but I can imagine that must have been difficult, especially since you had to work next to each other. Do you have assigned spaces here? If it had been me, I'd have wanted to be on the opposite side of the fairgrounds from someone who left me at the altar."

Wow, Hannah, way to come out, guns blazing. Her outraged expression kept me from patting myself on the back.

"Where did you hear that?"

Her eyes narrowed, and she looked around at the other vendors.

"The same place where I learned you're going to be a very rich woman. Congratulations. It's not every day you become a multi-millionaire."

"What?"

Her outraged shout was so loud that many people stopped to stare at us from the midway. Had I overplayed my hand?

"What are you talking about?"

This time, she dropped her tone down to a softer level and dropped the much-twisted towel onto the counter.

"You didn't know you were Tex's beneficiary? That his estate, minus what he left Pete, is worth millions?"

She put on a shocked face, but she still didn't make eye contact and a flush crept up her neck, staining her cheeks and jaw crimson.

"No. I didn't know that. Where did you hear that? Tex isn't even cold yet. How dare you go digging around like that? Wait... are you trying to accuse me?"

"Tex's attorney. He's already told the police, so I'm sure they'll have some questions for you as well."

I needed to get her honest reaction and so far; I wasn't buying the act of outrage. Once again, something didn't ring true about her performance.

"I don't even know what you're talking about. Isn't there going to be a reading of the will? I don't know how these things work."

"Typically, it's after the body is released for burial. In murder cases, however, the beneficiaries are usually looked at as potential suspects. Money is a powerful motive to want someone dead. So is the lack of money that was expected."

That got her to look at me. I could almost see the wheels of her brain turning as she leaned closer, motioning for me to do the same.

"You mean like an ex-wife who thought the money would go to her? Someone like Vera?"

"Perhaps. That brings up another question. Not only did you have your food truck parked next to a man who'd ended your engagement, you're also steps away from his ex-wife. How did that dynamic work?"

She snorted and picked the towel up, wringing it like the neck of a chicken.

"You've met Vera. How do you think it was? When we were together, it was worth it. I treasured every dirty look she shot me because it meant I'd won. Tex was a wonderful man. Giving. Honest. Sweet. If you ask me, she's the one who killed him. I thought it might have been Burt, but now... It had to be her. She's the only one who makes sense."

"Really? That's interesting. She didn't stand to gain much, besides the life insurance policy."

"Life insurance? I didn't know Tex had a life insurance policy."

"It was an old one. He likely forgot about it. But yes, she's the sole beneficiary."

"How much is it?"

I didn't like the way her eyes gleamed as she kept twisting the rag. Could she really not have known that Tex was worth a lot of money? That he'd changed his will to leave it all to her? It strained the bounds of credulity. Sheila was smart. She had to have known. Right?

"I don't know. You'll have to ask her."

"As if I'd do that. Well. You're positive that he named me in the will?"

"I am. I just read it a few hours ago. He left plenty of money for Pete to keep the truck running, but I don't know how that will pan out. Maybe he can hire someone."

"Pete's useless. Tex was the heart and soul of that food truck. Without Tex, Pete has nothing."

The awed look on her face had faded to one that bordered somewhere near disdain.

"If you'll forgive me for an impertinent question, is there that much money in food trucks? I mean, Tex's trailer is state-of-the art and he must have had a nice pickup to haul it back and forth, but that's a lot of money to leave behind."

"It was his wife's money. Well, from her life insurance policy. Tex never felt right about spending it after she died. He stuck it in a savings account and wouldn't talk about it. Just imagine. All those lovely piles of money, getting moldy in the bank. And the interest rates? Until a few years ago, they were practically negative."

My radar pinged, and I stood a little straighter. For someone shocked she was the beneficiary of Tex's money, she sure knew a lot about his finances.

"Why didn't you mention your relationship with Tex when we found him?"

She startled as I yanked her from an apparently rosy dream filled with dollar signs and percentage points. She sighed and rubbed at the counter again.

"You know how it is. Things didn't work out, and we went our separate ways. I tried not to think about it."

"You worked next to each other every weekend. How could you do that?"

"It wasn't easy, but I managed."

She tossed the towel away with surprising vigor and stood tall.

"I need to get back to work. I may have money on paper, but it's not in my bank account yet. I've got to get prepared for the next rush."

"Will you quit doing this once the estate is settled? It could take months."

Was that a flash of alarm in her brown eyes? It sure looked like it.

"Months?"

"At least six months to go through probate in Colorado. Even after that, it can take many months before everything is disbursed. It's not like life insurance. That can pay out around thirty days."

She looked away and blinked a few times.

"Huh. I didn't know that. You're sure?"

"Yes."

She heaved a sigh and pulled a container of onions out from the counter, staring at it as though it held the key to the universe.

"I didn't know that. Well, all the more reason for me to get back to the grind."

"I'll let you get back to work. Have you seen my cat, by any chance?"

She held onto the plastic container so hard the sides crackled, but she shook her head.

"Cat? Oh, that's right. No. I haven't."

She turned away and bustled around, grabbing containers of ingredients to restock them. I was about to walk away when I heard her call my name.

"Hannah? If you ask me, Vera did it. She hated Tex with a passion. Besides, you said she's the life insurance beneficiary? I'm sure she'd appreciate that payout. I've heard through the grapevine she's had some money troubles."

I gave her my full attention, and she walked closer.

"Really?"

"She's vile. Did you know she used to tell lies about me? When I was with Tex. All the time. I think Tex believed her. Even though he knew better. That's why we broke up. She got in there and poisoned his mind against me. For a little while, I thought things might change. That we might get back together, but she had her hooks in him. There was no use."

She shook her head sadly and stared at Tex's food truck.

"I'm sorry, Sheila. That had to be tough."

She snorted and wiped her hands on her apron.

"Yeah. You can't believe anything that woman says. If you ask me, she's the one who grabbed your cat."

My heart nearly stopped.

"Why? Why do you say that? What do you know?"

She took a step away from me, hands up in the air.

"Oh. I know nothing for sure. Just that she's the type of person to do something like that. Look, I've got to get back to work, okay?"

She turned her back on me again, but I stood there for a moment more, waiting for her to elaborate. I could tell my presence was unnerving her, but I wasn't sure why. Was it because she'd killed Tex and was shouldering the blame onto Vera? She'd seemed genuinely surprised that it would take so long to get the money, and still not very heartbroken that the man she'd supposedly loved was dead. I pushed away from the counter and walked back to the midway, mind spinning.

My feet carried me automatically back to Vera's tent. But instead of the surly Vera, I found myself face to face with Patty. She blanked her face as I approached and I had a feeling I was the last person she wanted to see.

"If you're looking for Vera, she's gone," she said, voice weary. "She won't be back today. She's got a terrible migraine. All this excitement has been terrible for her. She's a person who needs peace."

Of all the things I'd heard today, that rang the most false. If anything, Vera seemed like a woman who fed on drama. I remembered Patty was the one who said her sister had a place in Blanco Ridge, misleading me with a smile. A plan quickly whirred to life in my head.

"My friend over there," I said, turning to motion towards where Anastasia was standing in front of Burt's food truck. "She's a marvel with natural medicine. She's helped me with headaches before. I could bring her something to help. I know how hard it is to suffer from migraines."

Patty shook her head slowly.

"That's nice of you, but no. Vera wouldn't like that. She wouldn't want anyone to go to any trouble for her."

Another patently false statement. I smiled wider.

"But I insist. I'll be driving through all the RV parks later and it's no trouble at all to drop something off. Which one is she staying in? You know, since the place in Blanco Ridge is an empty lot?"

Any pretense at civility fell away from Patty like gossamer wings in the wind. Her eyes were full of malice as they met mine. I suddenly realized just how tall she was, and powerful. We hadn't thought a woman had the strength to drive a skewer through Tex's back, hitting his heart, but here was a woman who could've done it without breaking a sweat.

"No, thank you. Vera and I don't believe in that mumbo-jumbo BS, anyway. Get out of this tent."

My mouth felt dry as I nodded and backed away, not trusting her enough to turn my back on her. If Vera had Razzy, we needed to work quickly. All Patty needed to do was phone her sister and my little girl might never see the light of day again. I walked as fast as I could towards the parking lot. We needed to find Vera, and we needed to do it now.

16

*B*y the time I made it to the parking lot, I was practically incoherent as I tried to explain to Ben why we needed to leave right now. He gently took me by the shoulders, locked eyes with me, and patiently waited until I ran out of steam.

"Hannah, slow down. Take a deep breath. I'm not trying to be patronizing, honest. I just need to understand what's going on."

I tried to tamp down the irrational anger that flared brightly in my chest, and seeing the concern in his eyes helped. Well, mostly. I still wanted to be on the road, scouring every RV park in a fifty-mile radius, five minutes ago, but I knew he had a point. I took a deep breath and let it out, hoping that somehow I could inhale enough peace to see me through this.

"I'm positive Vera has Razzy. She's acting erratically and her sister basically threatened me. We've got to find her."

Ben nodded and pulled out his phone.

"Okay. We're going to do this the smart way. Let me mobilize everyone so we can cover more ground. We have a bunch of friends here who want to help."

I listened as he called Sam and convinced him to run a DMV

search on Vera's vehicles. I could hear Sam's familiar voice through the phone and shuddered out a breath. We were so lucky to have landed in a county where we knew the law enforcement. I could only imagine what someone who wasn't used to us would think of this situation.

Rudy crawled into my lap while Gus reared up on his hind legs, his whiskers tickling my cheek.

"We're gonna find her, lady. I can feel it in my whiskers and they never lie."

I didn't know what that meant, but I grasped the hope he was offering me with both hands. A knock on the window of my Blazer startled me, and I spotted Ashley on the other side of the glass.

"Anastasia and Robert are right behind me," she said as I rolled down the window. "I saw you sprint this way after talking to Patty and figured you had a hot lead. What's going on?"

I filled her in and by the time I was done, Ben had a list of plate numbers from Sam. He ended the call and handed the list over to me.

"This is everything they've got on her. I'll pull up all the camp-grounds near us and we can divide and conquer. Sam and Ray are going to follow us. Once we locate Vera, we're to call them so we have an official presence. Ashley, do you want to take a picture of that list so you have it handy?"

"Abso-fricking-lutely," she said, grabbing for her phone. "We're gonna nail this lady and get Razzy back. No one messes with my fur-niece."

Her words brought a smile to my face as Anastasia and Robert jogged up. Robert's white hair stood out like a beacon against his red face, while Anastasia looked cool as a cucumber, as usual. I didn't know how she did it.

Ashley took care of bringing them up to speed and we all split up into our separate vehicles. I had to move Rudy to buckle my seat belt as Ben fired up the engine with a grin.

"We're close, Hannah. Hang in there."

He took my hand in his as we sped out of the parking lot, leading our convoy of vehicles. Rudy joined Gus in the backseat, each taking a side so they could watch the scenery as we drove down the highway. Almost immediately, an RV park came into view and Ben pulled in, while our friends continued on. I crossed my fingers as we began cruising slowly past the gleaming row of RVs.

"They're so big," Rudy said. "How much do they cost?"

"Some of them cost more than a house," Ben said, letting out a low whistle as we rolled past a luxury fifth wheel camper with five slide-outs that dominated two spaces. "That one is probably close to half a million dollars."

"Wow," I said, blinking in shock. "I mean, it's nice to always have a place to stay when you're traveling, but that is a lot of money."

"I suppose a lot of these people sell their homes and live on the road. It's not for me, but I can see the allure of seeing the country at your own pace."

"It's kind of like a snail," Gus said, as he peered out the window. "Always lugging your home around."

I snorted as the mental picture of a luxury snail came to mind. He wasn't wrong. We came to the last row of campers and my shoulders sank, humor long forgotten. She wasn't here. Ben squeezed my hand as he navigated back out of the park.

"We'll try the next one."

Darkness crept over the landscape as we continued on the highway. The Sangre de Cristo mountains loomed closer, but I was too wrapped up in my worry to appreciate their beauty. I pulled up a map of the campgrounds on my phone to see how close we were to the next one.

"This one's only about a mile away, but I think that's the one Ashley's doing. Let's go to the one five miles from here."

Ben nodded and glanced to the side as a pickup flew past, narrowly avoiding a collision with oncoming traffic. I glimpsed the driver and passenger and straightened in my seat.

"Ben! That was Sheila and Patty! What are they doing?"

"I don't know, but she's in one heck of a hurry. Let's follow them. Call Ray and let him know."

I dialed Ray's number with shaking hands as Ben picked up

speed. It couldn't be a coincidence that they were out here, could it? Ray's familiar voice came on the line.

"Did you find her?"

"Not yet, but Sheila and Patty just came tearing past. We're following them."

"We're on our way. Do not engage, Hannah. Patty's got priors for deadly assault and many other offenses. I repeat, do not engage."

I signed off with a noncommittal murmur and looked at Ben.

"Did you hear that?"

"I did."

His face was set as he sped up.

"They all did it together, didn't they? The tall person in a black hoodie that Chrissie saw. It was Patty. It had to be."

"I think you're right, Hannah. But why?"

"Money. It was all about the money. You should've seen Sheila's face when I told her she'd have to wait for probate, while Vera would get the life insurance payout quickly. I should've known she was involved."

Ben pushed the Blazer to its limits, but it couldn't keep up with the high-powered truck. Patty was driving like a bat out of hell, and I didn't want to think about the reasons for their haste. The seconds dragged on as we turned a corner on the winding road and saw nothing but an empty road ahead.

"Where did they go?"

Ben said a terrible word as we looked around. I spotted a sign that made my heart race.

"There, Ben. It's a campground. I bet that's where Vera is."

He floored the Blazer and took a skidding turn that had me groping for the handle above the door as the cats in the backseat dug into their seats with their nails to stay upright. The road changed to gravel, and the Blazer slewed around while Ben struggled to regain control.

He shot me an apologetic glance before lowering his speed. I let out the breath I was holding and quickly called Ray.

"Ray, we're at the Eastern Crest campground. We're pretty sure they're here."

"We're a few minutes out, Hannah. Hang tight."

I could hear the roar of his engine through the phone line and nodded, even though he couldn't see me.

"Okay. Please, hurry."

I ended the call and fired off a quick text to Ashley, asking her to relay the message to our other friends. My hands were shaking so badly I could barely tap out the words. I looked up just in time to see the pickup we'd been following roaring back, nearly pushing us off the narrow dirt road. Patty's malevolent glare made my blood run cold in the split-second glance I caught from her before they passed us.

Ben slammed on the brakes and executed a perfect three-point turn to turn us around. Patty's truck kicked up so much dust it was nearly impossible to see as we started after them. I gripped Ben's arm as I dialed Ray again.

"They're leaving. We're still in pursuit. They just turned left on the highway."

"Who was in the pickup?"

"I saw Patty, but they passed us so quickly I couldn't see anyone else. I'm guessing they grabbed Vera."

"I'll have Sam peel off and check her camper while I continue on. Over and out."

Ray ended the call, and I stared ahead, just picking up the tail-lights of the pickup in the distance. There was a weak glow of sunshine on the western horizon, but the scrubby hills were turning black as the last light of the day fled.

"Where are they going?"

I looked at a sign as we flashed past and my stomach dropped.

"The only thing out here is the King Valley bridge. You don't think..."

I didn't finish my sentence. I couldn't. All I could think about was Razzy being suspended a thousand feet in the air above a raging river. What were they thinking? Ben took the corner into the park, following the lights, a grim expression on his face. We had to close the distance.

"Can cars go across this bridge?"

"I think so. But I thought it was only official park vehicles that may access it."

"Something tells me these women don't care about official rules."

As if to illustrate his words, we slowed as we passed an official-looking gate that was hanging off its hinges, destroyed by Patty's pickup's front end. I swallowed hard and gripped the sides of my seat as Ben sped on. A structure loomed in the distance, gleaming under bright lights.

"Is that the bridge?"

Rudy's voice was muffled in awe as we got closer. The bright lights on either side of the suspension bridge lit up the area, but the vast space underneath it remained black. The visitor center was dark and I couldn't tell if any employees were still around. I spotted Patty's pickup as they got closer.

"They're gonna cross it!"

Ben's face was stark white in the vehicle's darkness, lit by a sickly green glow from the dash. A loud horn sounded, drawing my attention back to the bridge. A man jumped out of his Jeep as Patty revved up her pickup, shoving aside the park vehicle with a shriek of metal on metal. The man clung to the side of the bridge, watching in horror as the pickup crossed it.

The bridge swayed slightly, forcing her to slow down to nearly a crawl. I opened my window, listening to the boards underneath the pickup as it rolled across. The man who'd leapt from the Jeep stood in the middle of the road, waving his arms.

"You've got to stop! No vehicles are allowed on the bridge! The police have already been called."

Ben rolled down his window and leaned out, shouting to be heard over the sound Patty's truck made on the bridge.

"Detective Ben Walsh. Those women are suspected of murder. The Chief of Police is right behind us. He knows we're here. Where does that road lead?"

"That's Route 50. It leads back into the mountains, but civilian vehicles aren't allowed to pass."

"I don't think they care," Ben said, a grim set to his face. "We have to follow. Please let Ray Weston know what's going on when he gets here."

Luckily, the man didn't ask to see Ben's badge. He merely nodded and thumped the door of the Blazer before stepping back, allowing us to cross. Sirens sounded in the distance and I noticed flashing lights coming from the hills across the bridge. Ray must have called in backup. The women were sandwiched between us, with nowhere to go.

Ben took a big breath as we rolled across the wooden planks slowly. The bridge swayed, and the contents of my stomach nearly ended up on my feet as the wind picked up. This was not safe, but I didn't care. I was certain my little girl was in that pickup and I would let nothing keep me from her.

Patty's pickup came to a halt. They must have seen the flashing lights up ahead. Ben stopped and let out a low groan as the bridge continued to sway. I glanced at him, alarmed to see a thin sheen of sweat over his face.

"Are you okay?"

"Fine."

He ground the words out between his teeth. He wasn't fine. Not by a long shot. I remembered his fear of heights and gripped his hand for support.

"It's going to be okay. This bridge is sturdy, even if it doesn't feel like it."

He nodded, refusing or unable to speak. Gus and Rudy crowded close, their whiskers tickling my arm.

"It's okay, man," Gus said, moving to slide into Ben's lap. "It's okay."

Ben's lip quirked up in a smile as the big Maine Coon consoled him. Rudy glanced at me, his blue eyes wide with fear. I gave him an encouraging nod before noticing the doors of the pickup ahead had opened, and the three women were getting out.

I opened my door, joining them on the wooden planks, remembering not to lock my knees as the bridge swayed in a sudden gust of wind.

"Hannah! What are you doing?"

I ignored Ben's plea and focused instead on the women in front of me. Sheila was gripping something to her chest, and I had a feeling I knew exactly what it was.

"Stop right there! Nobody move," Vera called out. "We demand safe passage across the bridge."

Sirens shattered the rest of her words and I risked a glance over my shoulder, spotting Ray as he slid to a stop behind us, not quite on the bridge. His voice crackled through the loudspeaker.

"You are surrounded, ladies. Give up or we'll add a host of other charges to the already long list you're already facing."

"I don't think so, Chief," Vera howled, her voice carrying in the wind. "We've got an ace in the hole. Show 'em, Sheila!"

The wind whipped through my hair as Sheila raised the bundle she was holding, dangling it off the side of the bridge. From their spot in the middle, the drop seemed endless. The bundle squirmed, and I shouted out a wordless cry of horror.

"No one move, or I'll drop the cat. I'll do it!"

Sheila's voice was unhinged as she dangled Razzy over the dizzying drop. I glanced hopelessly at Ben, seeing the horror I felt mirrored right back at me. Two cat-shaped shadows jumped out of my window, landing near my feet. I felt Rudy's fur brush my leg before he moved off, disappearing into the shadows on the far side of the bridge.

A bright light from Ray's car shone on the women, and my heart clenched painfully as I spotted Razzy's eyes blinking in the glare.

"Stop. We can talk about this, ladies."

"No talking!" Vera yelled. "You either call off the cops on the other side, or the cat goes."

I edged closer, wishing I had wings to narrow the distance. Razzy's eyes met mine and time slowed as Sheila made a face, screwing up her nose. Her face turned away and she let out a terrible sneeze at the same time Gus and Rudy let out twin infernal yowls that raised the hair on the back of my neck.

Time ground to a halt as Sheila's hands opened as she screamed. I ran, feeling as though my feet were trapped in cement as the bundle containing Razzy dropped. The only sound I could hear was the pounding of my heart.

17

hree things happened simultaneously. First, I moved faster than I ever would've thought possible. I moved towards Razzy as though my feet had wings. Second, Sheila let out a piercing scream that seemingly made time return to its normal speed, as Gus and Rudy plowed into her. Third, Ben somehow crossed the distance towards Sheila, making it to her just before I did. He shouldered her out of the way, knocking her off balance as he reached for Razzy. She went down hard on the wooden planks, still making that horrible shrieking sound.

Ben let out a shout as Razzy twisted mid-air, clinging to him with her claws, a terrified expression on her face. She clung to him as he hauled her over the railing. My legs nearly gave way as he cradled her to his chest. Gus and Rudy growled, low and deep, pinning Sheila to the bridge, white as she sobbed in terror.

The truck's engine roared to life, and I looked up to see the tail-lights moving as Patty floored it. The wooden planks rattled as she fishtailed before gaining control and shooting ahead. Right then, I didn't care if they got away. Razzy was in my arms and the woman who'd threatened her with certain death was cowering in front of us.

Ben passed Razzy over to me and she scrabbled her claws against my shirt as she tried to get as close as she could to me. As he let her go, I saw blood from Razzy's claws running down his arms.

"Mama, mama, it's okay. I'm okay. Don't let them get away! Their murderers and cat-nappers! Ben, I'm so sorry I scratched you. I'm so sorry."

A huge smile spread over Ben's face as he stroked her head, while her words tumbled out so quickly they were almost incomprehensible.

"You didn't mean it, little one. I'm glad you didn't fall. I thought for a second..."

He didn't need to finish his sentence. We all knew what he thought. What we'd all thought in that horrible moment where Razzy's life hung in the balance. I held her as tightly as I could without hurting her.

"You're safe, baby girl. You're safe."

Her little heart pounded so hard I could feel it through her fur. Ray cleared his throat and approached, gun at the ready.

"Sheila Bream, put your hands up."

She cringed as Gus and Rudy stared her down, fur fluffed, making them look even bigger than they actually were. I'd known Gus could handle himself. After all, he'd lived life as a feral cat before finding Ben, but Rudy was a surprise. His sweet face was pulled back into a vicious snarl as he stared at the woman cowering underneath him.

"Get them off me! Get them off me! I'll do anything but get them off me!"

Gus and Rudy eased away from the woman slowly, never stopping the growls rumbling deep within their chests.

Ray gave them a wide berth as he skirted around Sheila, never taking his weapon off her. He rummaged with his free hand at his belt and tossed something over to Ben.

"Cuff her."

Ben nodded and heaved Sheila up on her feet before turning her and closing the cold steel around her wrists. My heart began slowing down, and I took a shaky breath. I wanted nothing more than to take Razzy somewhere safe and cuddle her until she fell asleep, safe in my arms. Sheila babbled, still staring at the boys as they circled her feet, growling terribly.

"Get them away from me! My God, these beasts aren't natural. Save me!"

I rolled my eyes before softly calling to Gus and Rudy. They backed towards me, fur still fluffed.

"What's unnatural is a woman threatening a poor, innocent cat with death, just to save her sorry hide."

Ray shot him a look and Ben stepped away, hands up in the air.

"I did nothing, okay? I'm innocent. Patty asked me to go with her in the truck to get Vera. I had nothing to do with Tex's murder. I am an innocent bystander. I didn't know they'd done it until they started talking about in the car. I tell you, I'm innocent!"

For a moment, I almost believed her. Her eyes were wide as she looked at Ray, the wind whipping through her hair. Almost. But not quite. Something rang false, somewhere within her words. Razzy squiggled in my arms before whispering.

"She's lying. All three of them did it. Vera bragged about with Patty last night. They were so certain they were going to get away. Sheila was the one who distracted him. Vera's the one who planned it. Patty drove the poker through his back. They were framing Sheila so they could get away."

I'd heard enough. There was no way I was going to let Sheila get away with this. I cleared my throat and raised my voice.

"That's not true, is it, though? Tex was a big man. Tall enough that you couldn't do the job yourself. Nor could Vera. You needed help. Help from Patty. Her hand might have held the weapon, but the one you used was worse. You distracted him while Patty snuck up behind him. Tell the truth, Sheila. We know everything."

Her eyes went even wider, confirming Razzy's words. She shook her head and looked back at Ray.

"She's lying. There's no way you can prove it. I loved Tex! I'd never hurt him. We were going to get back together. Vera couldn't handle it. I'd made the mistake of telling her about the will and she went crazy. I swear to you, Ray Weston, I'm innocent. Let me go."

"Now I don't think I need to do anything, except book you for suspicion of murder and felony eluding of a police officer."

"Don't forget animal cruelty," Ben said, his face hard in the glow of the headlights beaming across the bridge. "That charge alone carries eighteen months in prison. You deserve more than that."

Ray nodded and motioned for Sheila to move. The radio pinned to his shoulder crackled to life, and I heard Sam's voice.

"We got 'em, Chief. Patty put up a fight, but we got them."

"Bring 'em in, son," Ray said with a wintry smile before removing his finger from the handset button. "I can't wait to see how quickly you three turn on each other. Colorado might not have the death penalty, but you're all looking at many years behind bars."

Sheila licked her lips, shooting an anxious glance over her shoulder as Ray pushed her ahead. "But when I get out, I'll still have the life insurance money, right? I'll still have that?"

Ray shook his head and let out a sardonic laugh.

"Sounds like you don't know about the Slayer Law. Even if you three somehow get the charges reduced to manslaughter, you've forfeited that payout, Sheila. The money will go to the second named beneficiary. So long as they weren't involved, too."

She let out a low cry that sounded like a wounded animal as Ray propelled her towards his vehicle. Ben breathed in through his nose and checked around for Gus and Rudy. They were sticking close, each had a paw on his shoe.

"Come on, guys. Let's get off this bridge and get you home."

You'd never have known he was terrified of heights as he led us back across the swaying bridge. While I didn't share that fear, I couldn't help holding onto Razzy a little tighter as we rushed back towards the Blazer. If I never set foot on another suspension bridge, that would be just fine with me.

I kept her in my arms as Ben opened the door for us. Gus and

Rudy vaulted inside, crowding around as I crawled into the passenger seat. Ben carefully shut the door and walked around the front end. By the time he was back in the driver's seat, Ray had backed up enough to let us get off the bridge.

Ben never took his eyes off the rearview mirror as we backed up. His hands held the steering wheel so tightly they blanched completely white. My phone rang through the hands-free system, making us all jump. Ben glanced at me and I nodded, motioning for him to push the button to connect the call.

"Did you find her? We've all heard the sirens. We're up by the visitor center."

"We've got her, Ash. We'll be there in a few. I'll tell you about it then."

I motioned for Ben to end the call before burrowing my face into Razzy's soft fur. She started purring, gently at first, before ramping up the rumbles to near deafening levels. My little girl was back where she belonged, in my arms, and thankfully, she looked fine, at least on the exterior. I had no doubt, though, that inside, she was going to have some emotional stress from her ordeal.

Rudy's whiskers tickled my arm as he gently sniffed Razzy's fur.

"You smell like the disinfectant I smelled on Vera!"

Razzy turned so she could look at him and they gently touched noses while Gus looked on with troubled eyes. Rudy backed away so Gus could have his turn at greeting her. They murmured to one another, whiskers meshing together into an intricate weave of love.

"I'm so glad you're back."

"Me too."

I took a shaky breath, tears ready to spill yet again, and noticed Ben's eyes were rather damp as well. He reached across to stroke Razzy's fur before focusing back on the road. I shifted her in my arms so I could look at her face.

"You're sure you're okay? She didn't hurt you?"

Razzy shook her head and looked at me with so much love it nearly took my breath away.

"No. She fed me and made sure I had clean water and a clean box. For a murderer, she was surprisingly decent. She had me locked in a tiny bathroom, but she made sure there was a soft bed. Not that I used it," Razzy said, tossing her head. "I wouldn't be bribed. It wasn't bad. Not as bad as it could've been, I guess."

"Why did she take you? Did she say?"

"She knew you were getting close to figuring it out. She figured if you were gone, your focus would shift and you'd stop investigating. I'm glad you didn't, Mama. I knew you'd keep going. I'm a tough cat. I can take care of myself. I was waiting for her to let her guard down so I could get away and come find you. I had a plan to dart past her the next time she opened the door, but she was too quick for me."

I thought about the many miles that separated the campground from the fairgrounds, let alone our apartment, and shuddered. Even if she had gotten free, the odds of her braving the many dangers and miles would've been small. She put a soft paw up to my face and gave me a head butt.

"It doesn't matter how far, Mama. I will always find you."

The tears I'd been holding back broke free, and I sobbed my heart out as I held her to my chest. Ben pulled the Blazer alongside Ashley's car in the parking lot and eased out, after giving Razzy a quick kiss on the head. I could hear him talking to our friends as I got myself under control.

"I'm so glad we found you, Razzy. I don't know what I'd do without you. You're everything to me. You all are."

Rudy and Gus somehow clambered into my lap, pinning me under their collective weight as they snuggled with Razzy. I sat there, awash in love, and looked out the window towards the distance, where I could see Ray's headlights in the distance.

If justice was served, the three women would go away for a very long time. I had no doubt they'd turn on one another, and Sheila would be forced to tell the truth to save her hide. My mind briefly touched on Tex and I sent a glance upwards, wishing him peace. I'd never met him, but he certainly didn't deserve to go out the way he had. With any luck, we could at least close the last chapter of his life and make sure the people who killed him were brought to justice.

Razzy shifted in my lap, her claws briefly gripping my leg, but I didn't mind. My mind flashed back to that awful moment when she could've fallen, and I sent a silent thank you up to the heavens. She was back home where she belonged, and there was no way I was letting her out of my sight.

18

A knock on the window interrupted the cats' cuddle puddle on my lap, and all three sat bolt upright, whiskers flared, until they saw it was Ashley on the other side. I rolled down the window so she could fuss over Razzy.

"Baby girl, you don't know how worried we were about you. Your mama has been frantically trying to trace you down."

Razzy raised herself up onto her hind legs, head butting Ashley's hand before giving her a swift lick that made my friend smile.

"Razzy, the newspaper staff printed up flyers to help find you. Even Vinnie helped," I said.

Her eyes widened as she turned to me.

"Even Vinnie?"

"Yep. You're adored, sweetheart."

Razzy purred so loudly I was positive you could have heard her three counties over. I noticed the conversation died down around my friends and craned my head out of the window. Ray was approaching and his face was serious. Anastasia glanced at me and I got the message. I patted Razzy, hating that I needed to get out and leave her in the car.

"Okay, guys. I've gotta go talk to Ray. I'll be right outside, though."

Typically, Razzy would've rolled her eyes, but this time? This time, she gripped my arm tightly before letting me go with a nod. The boys hopped into the backseat and I moved her into the driver's seat so I could get out.

"I'll be right back. I'll keep the window down so you can hear everything."

She nodded, eyes enormous in her face as she kneaded the fabric on the seat below her. My brows knit, recognizing that she was under a great deal of stress. I needed to get her home as quickly as possible. I slid out and slowly closed the door, turning to face Ray and my friends.

"I'm taking her in," Ray said as soon as he noticed me. "But I wanted to check with you on a few things before I did. I heard what you said to her, that Vera planned the whole thing and Patty was the murderer. How did you know that?"

I was stuck. I couldn't say that Razzy told me after overhearing the women talking. I wished I could, since it would make it so much easier to have had an eyewitness on the inside. The women wouldn't have a chance in court with Razzy as the star witness. Unfortunately, it couldn't happen, no matter how much I wanted it to. I hated lying, but I had to figure out a way to tell him the truth without revealing my abilities.

"It was a hunch. When I told her it could take months to get the proceeds from Tex's estate, she looked panicked. I'd noticed each time I talked to her, Sheila tried to pin the murder on someone else. First it was Pete. Then it was Burt. And finally, she pointed the finger at Vera. Something about her never added up, though. I guess it was just instinct that led me to believe she played a part in it."

Ray looked at me for so long I had to physically restrain myself from squirming. Ben looked uncomfortable, but tried to hide it. How well did Ray know him? All it would take was one look at Ben's face to know the truth - if he knew how Ben reacted to things.

"I see. Well, you've got a powerful hunch system going for you, Hannah. Luckily, the physical evidence we found backs up your claim. We got a partial print on that earring, putting Vera at the scene. The scrap of fabric you found matches up with an apron found in Sheila's truck. The only one we don't have any direct evidence on is Patty."

"I'm certain that's who Chrissie saw running through the back of the food trucks that morning."

"You are most likely right," Ray said, taking off his cowboy hat to scratch his scalp. "On the plus side, Sheila's already tripping over herself, trying to get a deal. I think by morning, we'll have enough to charge everyone and lock them up. Your cat's okay?"

I glanced back towards the Blazer, where I saw the cats lined up, staring out the window, hanging on Ray's every word.

"She's been through a lot, but no physical harm."

"Well, that's good. I'll need to get some statements from you both, but that can wait until tomorrow. You won't need to come back down, though. A phone interview will suffice. I'm sure you're more then ready to get back to your stomping grounds."

I nodded and a little of the tension coiling through my shoulders relaxed.

"Thanks, Chief."

He nodded, clapped Ben on the back, and walked away. He got about five feet before he turned. A smirk curled his lips up to one side.

"If I didn't know better, I'd think there was something very special about those cats of yours. I sure wish they could talk. It would make my job a lot easier."

He dipped his cowboy hat before turning. The five of us held our collective breath until he got in his vehicle and pulled away.

"That was close," Ashley said, putting a hand to her chest. "If he'd asked one more question, I would've been singing like a bird."

Anastasia patted her arm and smiled.

"I think he knows more than he's saying, but he also knows that no one would believe him. He's a good man with a good heart. Even if he knows our secret, it's in safe hands with him."

She was right. Ray Weston was a wonderful man and an honest police officer. We'd lucked out that we'd ended up in his jurisdiction.

Anastasia walked closer to me and smoothed my flyaway hair from around my face.

"She's going to be fine, Hannah. She's more resilient than you know. Keep her close and she'll recover."

I didn't bother asking how Anastasia knew my secret fears. Somehow, she always did. Instead, I folded her into a hug and whispered my thanks. She stepped away and walked over to Razzy, leaning against the car door.

"Well, Razzy girl. You found your way home. I'm glad you're okay. We'd all be lost without you."

She stroked Razzy's head, and I watched as Razzy's eyes closed blissfully under Anastasia's hand. I absurdly wished for the tea set Anastasia kept in her back room to put an end to this night. However she made her tea, it usually brought me peace. Anastasia smiled and winked before going back to Robert.

I felt Ben's strong arm close around my waist and suddenly, all the exhaustion from the past two days finally caught up with me. All I wanted to do was sleep with Razzy cuddled in my arms.

"Let's get everyone home. We can worry about all of this tomorrow."

I nodded and leaned into him while we said our goodbyes to our friends. Ashley gave me a rib-cracking hug before flying back to her vehicle, eager to get home to Grace and Dan. Anastasia waved as Robert pulled out of the parking lot, leaving us alone underneath the bright lights.

"We did it," I said, almost doubting what had just taken place. "We found her and we caught the killers. I can't believe it."

Ben pressed a kiss on the top of my head before steering me towards the Blazer. I climbed in, fastened my seat belt, and held open my arms for Razzy to crawl in my lap. Ben looked at all of us before turning on the car.

"Is everyone okay with going home tonight or do you want to stay in a hotel? It's about an hour's drive from here."

Razzy's voice was sleepy as she answered.

"Home. I just want to go home. I'm not sure I'll ever want to leave those four walls again."

I glanced at Ben in alarm as he backed out of our parking spot. That wasn't like my little adventurous cat. He shook his head slightly, and I stroked the fur on her back. Honestly, after what she'd been through, I couldn't blame her.

We drove on in a comfortable silence for many miles while Razzy snoozed in my lap. She twitched a few times, but a soft word eased her sleep. We were about halfway home when she sat up and yawned widely.

"That's better. Say, I never got my fried chicken," she said, sounding quite put out. "Or pictures of the baby goats."

A stunned silence filled the vehicle for a moment before we all started laughing. You couldn't keep Razzy down. All the stress I'd been holding onto finally evaporated as I laughed so hard tears ran down my cheeks. At least this time, they were tears of happiness. I'd had enough sad tears to last me years.

I finally got control of myself while Razzy grumbled on my lap.

"I don't think it was *that* funny. Fried chicken is a very serious thing."

"Razzy, we'll get you your own bucket of chicken after what you've been through."

Rudy's eyes gleamed in the light from the dashboard as he leaned forward.

"A bucket is an awful lot of chicken. But don't worry, Razzy. I'll help."

That sent us off again, and the remaining miles flew by as we headed home. I looked out the window as the cats began bickering over who could eat more fried chicken, and whether mashed potatoes were better than corn. A feeling of rightness settled on my shoulders as I listened. We were all back together.

Ben glanced over and took my hand, his look gentle.

"You holding up okay over there?"

I nodded before leaning my head back against the headrest.

"Absolutely. I might ask for an extra day off tomorrow, though. I think I'll be able to sleep for a week."

Razzy snuggled into my chest.

"I'm going to do the same. Razzy, do you want to talk more about what happened?" Ben asked, glancing over at her before looking back at the road. "Sometimes it helps to talk about it."

"We'll help you play Tetris," Rudy said, pawing at my arm. "I read that's supposed to help with trauma recovery."

Razzy blinked at him before looking at me.

"I don't. Not right now. Maybe later. Right now, I just want to enjoy being where I belong. I'm tougher than I look."

I glanced back at Gus and he nodded his head slightly. I knew between all of us, Razzy would have the support she needed. If she didn't want to talk about it right now, that was fine. We'd have time in the days ahead to go through everything.

"You mentioned seeing Eden," Razzy said, twisting so she could look at me full on. "We should do that. I have a feeling she's going to need us."

"Yeah!" Rudy said, bouncing in place. "I want to say hi to Jasper and see Luna's kits."

Razzy's eyes narrowed at the mention of the beautiful white cat who'd once been intent on making Gus her mate. Her whiskers drooped slightly.

"Yes. Of course. But back to Eden. I think we should go as soon as we can."

I shared a glance with Ben, but I couldn't deny Razzy anything. Apparently, her plans for staying home forever were already long gone. That was more like my little girl.

"If you're okay with going on a trip, that's fine. We'll get it booked."

She nodded and settled back down, yawning again.

"Good. Wake me when we've got the chicken."

I chuckled and grabbed my phone out of my pocket to place an order we could pick up. Within a few minutes, we'd be back home. Even though we'd still be dealing with the fallout from Tex's murder and her kidnapping, that could wait. That was tomorrow. Tonight? Tonight was all about celebrating. I hit the button to complete my order and smiled over at Ben.

"Let's go get our little girl her chicken."

"That's the best thing I've heard all night," he said, winking at Razzy.

I stroked her back while he turned off the highway. Questions about why she was so insistent about seeing Eden swirled in my mind, but those could wait, too. Something told me we'd have plenty of time to figure out our next adventure.

DON'T MISS A FUN CROSSOVER!

Can't get enough of Razzy and the boys? They'll be making a special guest appearance in the next Clowder Cats book and then they'll have a new adventure all their own right after that!

Pushing Up Daisies - A Clowder Cats Cozy Mystery Book #4

At long last, Spring has arrived at the Valewood Resort, and Eden Brooks couldn't be happier. Wildflowers are blooming and business is booming. After a rough few months at the resort, finally, everything is going right.

Eden teams up with a local mountain guide to provide wildflower tours to guests of the resort. Just when things couldn't get any better... they get worse.

One of her tour guests ends up dead, and unfortunately, way too many people have a motive, including the mountain guide she hired. Eden gets tangled up in a web of deception, full of false starts, lies, and misdirection.

Luckily, some of Eden's special friends are visiting, because she's going to need all the help she can get to catch this killer, before she ends up pushing up daisies, too.

Don't Miss a Fun Crossover!

Fans of the Razzy Cat Cozy Mysteries will love this crossover! Coming in early Fall of 2024!

A NEW SERIES! MILLIE THE MIRACLE CAT COZY MYSTERY SERIES

Olivia Sutton just moved to Timber Falls, a little town hidden in the mountains of Colorado, with the goal of starting fresh and leaving her past firmly in the rearview mirror. She's got a plan and some hard-earned savings. How hard could starting over be?

While she's scouting locations to start a new bookstore, she discovers a bedraggled stray cat, and something far more sinister.

Will the people in her newly claimed hometown believe she's innocent? Is she losing her grip on reality or is her new cat capable of strange things?

Join Olivia and Millie the Cat as they work together to save Olivia's reputation, find a killer, and begin living their new lives.

Order Your Copy Now!

HAVE YOU READ THE CLOWDER CATS SERIES YET?

Shireen 'Eden' Brooks is ready for a fresh start. Thanks to her friend, Hannah Murphy, and some special cats, that's exactly what she's going to get.

She's got a brand new job at an all-inclusive resort. Life is looking up, until one guest can't check out... Eden's going to need all the help she can get to solve this case, even if it comes from a very unexpected place.

If you liked Courtney McFarlin's Razzy Cat Cozy Mystery series, you'll love this adorable spin-off with some beloved characters from The Crisis at the Wedding who finally get to tell their own stories!

Get your copy now!

BOOKS BY COURTNEY MCFARLIN

A Razzy Cat Cozy Mystery Series

The Body in the Park

The Trouble at City Hall

The Crime at the Lake

The Thief in the Night

The Mess at the Banquet

The Girl Who Disappeared

Tails by the Fireplace

The Love That Was Lost

The Problem at the Picnic

The Chaos at the Campground

The Crisis at the Wedding

The Murder on the Mountain

The Reunion on the Farm

The Mishap at the Meeting

The Bones on the Trail

The Dispute at the Fair

The Commotion at the Race - Winter 2024

A Soul Seeker Cozy Mystery

The Apparition in the Attic

The Banshee in the Bathroom

The Creature in the Cabin

The ABCs of Seeing Ghosts

The Demon in the Den

The Ether in the Entryway

The Fright in the Family Room

The Ghoul in the Garage

The Haunting in the Hallway

The Imp at the Ice Rink

The Jinn in the Joists

The Kelpie in the Kennel

The Lady in the Library - Fall 2024

The Clowder Cats Cozy Mystery Series

Resorting to Murder

A Slippery Slope

A Mountain of Mischief

Pushing Up Daisies - Fall 2024

Millie the Miracle Cat Cozy Mystery Series

A New Beginning

Stacked Against Us

A Siren's Song Paranormal Cozy Mystery Series

The Wrong Note

A Major Case

Escape from Reality Cozy Mystery Series

Escape from Danger

Escape from the Past

Escape from Hiding

A NOTE FROM COURTNEY

Thank you for taking the time to read this novel. If you enjoyed the book, please take a few minutes to leave a review. As an independent author, I appreciate the help!

If you'd like to be first in line to hear about new books as they are released, don't forget to sign up for my newsletter. Click here to sign up! https://bit.ly/2H8BSef

A LITTLE ABOUT ME

Courtney McFarlin currently lives in the Black Hills of South Dakota with her fiancé and their two cats.

Find out more about her books at:
   www.booksbycourtney.com

Follow Courtney on Social Media:

https://twitter.com/booksbycourtney

https://www.instagram.com/courtneymcfarlin/

https://www.facebook.com/booksbycourtneym

Made in the USA
Middletown, DE
25 June 2024

56306561R00099